Nameless

Elle Pepper

Phoenix Voices Publishing

Copyright © 2024 by Elle Pepper

All rights reserved.

No part of this publication may be reproduced, distributed, or transmitted in any form or by any means, including photocopying, recording, or other electronic or mechanical methods, without the prior written permission of the publisher, except as permitted by U.S. copyright law. For permission requests, contact Phoenix Voices Publishing, 7901 4th St. N, St. Petersburg, FL, 33702, 727-222-0090.

The story, all names, characters, and incidents portrayed in this production are fictitious. No identification with actual persons (living or deceased), places, buildings, and products is intended or should be inferred.

Elle Pepper asserts the moral right to be identified as the author of this work.

Elle Pepper has no responsibility for the persistence or accuracy of URLs for external or third-party Internet Websites referred to in this publication and does not guarantee that any content on such Websites is, or will remain, accurate or appropriate.

Designations used by companies to distinguish their products are often claimed as trademarks. All brand names and product names used in this book and on its cover are trade names, service marks, trademarks, and registered trademarks of their respective owners. The publishers and the book are not associated with any product or vendor mentioned in this book. None of the companies referenced within the book have endorsed the book.

Dedication	1
Forward	2
Translation Circuit On	5
Rican	7
A New Mandate	17
The Decision	21
Cult of N4m31355	26
Called Up	32
Ambushed	37
Captain's Log	42
Security	45
Best Pilot	51
The Man Called Magic	58
Medicine	66
Old Friends	75

Old Enemies	79
Maiden Voyage	85
Walker of the Sands	94
Nameless	99
Conversations	106
Strange	110
The Dream of the Walker	117
Captain's Log	119
Sabotage, Sabotage	121
Security	125
AJ	128
Double Trouble	131
Captain's Log	138
The Real Man	139
Once an Avenger	141
tick tick tick	143
The Planet	147
Statues	160
The Living Stone	162
Fallen	168
The Story of the First	174
Aftermath	187

Quarantine Log	193
Captain's Log	195
About the Author	197

To Ken Kuhlken. ADIOS!

Forward

Chronologically speaking, this book happens early in the timeline. This is after the war, but before the USL, the planetary government of Earth has become solid. They are about to hold their first elections after the revolution that got rid of the OSU or "Ground" patrol. The patrol itself has been disbanded except on Terra itself. On Earth, or Terra, as the snowy wreck is now called, they have the authority to enforce the law, and they can conscript anyone to do it.

Among these conscripts are "Units" or "Black Tunics" dressed entirely in black, they are seen as not just non-human but they are treated like robots and furnishings, they are deemed to be non-sentient and thereby are not allowed to marry, carry money, have children or basically do anything that is not part of their job.

While technically they can be reinstated after being a Black Tunic, it has never happened. Once they are stripped of their rights, they never get them back. Some places refuse to adhere to the Black Tunic codes and are actively pushing to have them repealed.

Among those races is the Girati. These space-faring people live in gigantic Generation ships and because they spend so little time in gravity, they age so slowly that a man or woman of over a hundred is just shy of middle age. The farther 'out' towards the rift they go, the more likely they will be to have trouble acclimating as a human.

Raised with a strict moral code that forbids killing without absolute necessity, and requires prayers and obligations for the dead, they are a close-knit community of travelers.

The easiest way to tell a spacer is to watch how they move. If a man stands straight and walks solidly, he or she is not space-born. The spacers stand lightly, shoulders rolled, and knees bent in case the gravity should fail and they have to kick off.

Among the Races of the USL, the three most superstitious that are commonly seen are related. The Kin, those who live in the snows of Terra, the Girati, who fly the stars, and Keepers of the way, sometimes called "Shedda" or "Singer of Sand" all three groups trace their lineage back to Earth before the "Great War" in this case, the Galactic War.

The OSU at this point in history is still fighting to regain what they have lost, and are convinced that they will rise again. But their xenophobic tendencies is why they were overthrown in the first place, they had boiled 'human' down to a few dozen sets of base pairs. And anyone not found within those sets was considered to be less than they were, inhuman, and unworthy of entry into their select club.

Unfortunately, the strict adherence to the base pair law nearly killed the Human race, as they teetered, perilously close to not having any genetic diversity. Those considered not 'pure' took to ships and left. The first to leave was the PC, the "Psychic Conglomerate" a group of humans gifted with Psychic ability and limited prescience to whom the Girati trace their lineage.

These ships, called by the Girati "First Fleet" or the "First Ships" were said to have vanished into the rift at the end of the galaxy and returned a thousand years later, while only a hundred had passed for the rest of the worlds. (That at least is the story told among the Girati, and the rift is known for Time Dilation, so that much is true.) How much of this is fiction, we don't know. We do know that only a few of the First Fleet came back and when they did, they were changed, it was their voyage in the rift that turned them into the Girati, that much all stories hold, but how where and why they came to have the Stones that run their ship, no one, not even the Girati remember.

Translation Circuit On

Duty log: USLS 2019, No name
    Captain: Tyrell Hanson.
    What follows is the true and complete log of the incident called "Nameless," and what follows is hereby classified deep black. The circumstances of the aforesaid incident are not to be discussed outside the members of the crew. No government official has clearance to discuss this without both Captain Hanson and Major Hunter in attendance.
    Furthermore, the incidents after the launch shall not appear in any file, redacted or not. Under authority of the charter, nor shall any action mentioned in this account be counted against those of the crew unless they have been charged with a crime under the statute of law. And then only the incidents by which their guilt or innocence may be known will be given, all other actions so noted will not be held against any party.
    Furthermore, though the accolades and awards stand, there is to be no mention of the incident in official record or file. Just a verification number so that future commands may know that the accolades and awards are true and correct but the incident

in question has been officially disavowed by any member of the government without clearance to speak.

Furthermore, it is hereby written that Pilot Abigail Hughes is awarded the Meritorious cross, the silver star for gallantry, and the Galactic award for duty to her ship and crew in the face of immeasurable danger. All of these are to be awarded posthumously, and her husband will also be recognized by the colonial star with cluster for his bravery in saving her life.

Furthermore, the incident which gave her the injury heretofore mentioned, and that killed her husband shall be investigated, and any found to be in violation shall pay under penalty of law. Her true and living kin shall be given her inheritance, and in her name, a likely pilot candidate will be inducted into the Academy from a colony world where they would not otherwise be able to enter due to poverty or class status on their world.

Her dead name shall be stricken forthwith from all documents, and reports, any filed under the improper name will be sent back with the notice, "No such being."

The account that follows is true and as complete as the data and memory allow.

Rican

THE AIR WAS ACRID, the fans, condensers, and regulators were offline, leaving the stench of burned skin and hair mingling with the scent of scorched metal and plastic as the ship shook again.

The Weapons array was offline and now they had been given the, "come to and prepare to be boarded" speech. He'd be damned if he'd let these upstart separatists have his ship.

"Abandon ship!" He yelled at the two surviving officers on the bridge. Most of the rest of the crew were dead, dying, or already gone. His ship, this ship, was named for his father, and he was going down with it, better than rotting in some prison for the next forty cycles, if he lived long enough to get there.

"But sir." Not that Ergan wanted to die, but he certainly didn't want to be accused of desertion. So he had to at least pretend to make a protest. He was only here because they conscripted him, forcing him into service with the last people he ever wanted to serve with.

"That's an order. Abandon ship, I'm going to scuttle her."

The young officer, he hadn't taken time to learn the name of, he'd only been on the ship a week, ran without so much as a 'yes sir' or a salute, it figured, "he's a colonial, probably threw in with separatists."

A few minutes later, the captain was the only crew member on the ship. With the engines locked and the helm being controlled from the bridge, there was nothing else to do. He was going to send her into the atmosphere and let her burn up on the way down. He thought that there was no one who could stop him. OSU ships, however, had a serious flaw. If you were small enough, the ship couldn't lock onto you. But you had to be very small, not much bigger than a human person, really. But if you were really lucky, really fast, and slightly insane, you could get past the sensors and onto the ship.

Only one vehicle was both small enough and fast enough to work, Gravity Boards, often called 'glide boards' able to be ridden down like a parachute. They would keep them at speed, but allow a controlled descent.

And of course, air tech helped too, in this case, Atmo bands. Capable of producing a bubble of air around the wearer and changing the gravity, they were a spacer's best friend. All this took only minutes when executed flawlessly by the only IRT brave enough to do it. And it was done well before the sensors registered. Which is why Captain Rican didn't know the IRT was there until he started getting hull breaches.

One in engineering, one in the corridor outside the bridge. The door was sealed, but it wouldn't take long for them to override it. If he had known who they were, he would have been afraid, but he just saw them as blips on the screen. But it wasn't until the door opened, under its own power, that he became afraid. Most IRT would just blow the lock and force the door open, but these guys hacked the door, or, more likely, just overrode it.

They were a legend to both sides, crazy enough to glide board onto a ship to keep her out of the atmosphere, but cleared enough to force open a locked door with a few keystrokes and a passkey.

It had taken them less than five minutes to override the locks, something that shouldn't be possible, especially on a ship at defense condition Alpha. And they came streaming in.

First came the king of Hearts, then came a pixie, then came Orion, the god for whom the constellation was named, and then; then came the leader, the grim reaper himself.

These were not costumes or low-grade holos. These were Glams. The name reserved for the most high-tech holo-skins available. They moved seamlessly and you could even touch the wearer and not disrupt it. The eyes blinked, the mouths moved, and in all ways the glam reacted like human skin. A holo-skin had somewhere between four and fifty-four hours of use time, depending on the model. The captain couldn't take his eyes off of them, telling them to get off his bridge. They made no reply, or even acknowledgement of him being there. It was only his good fortune he didn't rise to meet or attack them.

They entered in twos, a half-second apart, fanning out from the door, point and guard around the room, checking the bodies and keeping the captain covered with energy weapons. There were never less than two weapons pointed at him as they walked around the room, checking behind consoles and taking their places.

They all walked like spacers, but the Grim Reaper most of all, hands pulled in, shoulders rolled, knees bent, ready to kick off. It was a habit borne of long practice in space. There was little doubt between that, and the red crystal the creature wore, that under the hologram was a Girati.

The team worked seamlessly; they spoke carefully with the ease of long practice, and there were no names, just handles.

And as he sat there, watching them swarm his bridge, Captain Rican got the sinking feeling he knew *just* who these insane people were. Led by a Girati no one ever saw, bearing the handle Reaper, and the way they had boarded the ship without warning, led him to the possibility, but the clincher was the language, something that wouldn't translate. A language known only by the team. This could be none other than the Avengers. The legendary Black Pack. As far as insertion and retrieval teams went, these guys were a cut above.

They were fast, lucky, crazy and very, very good at their jobs. These were the people you called when there was no one else. There were more than the ones he saw here, he knew that, but they practiced squad routine, breaking into smaller groups as needed. He figured just as many were in engineering, and maybe a few in the bays to make sure no shuttles could be launched. It took less than two minutes for them to secure the bridge.

After two had sat down at the con stations, moving the bodies of the dead carefully and pausing to say a prayer for them, one of the figures finally spoke, reaching up to their collar to make sure the translator was working. "He's the only life form sir." It was the first phrase in Standard.

Standard had once been English, or so they said, but now it sounded like English learned by someone who first learned Russian, Chinese and Farsi. The dialect the Grim Reaper spoke was more musical, another nod to his Girati heritage. The captain didn't move. In fact, he barely dared to breathe. He'd heard the stories of the Grim Reaper and his crew. They were good, damn good, and damn lucky, too. And they didn't hesitate to do whatever it took within their code of morals to get the job done. While they were not pacifists, they were also not people who killed anyone they met. But if you pissed them off, they could make your life more miserable than it already was. And they were known for 'accidents' that lead to non- permanent injury of those who tried to run.

Reaper nodded.

"Good, shields up, pitch us up to bounce and grab onto something." It seemed the man noticed the Captain for the first time. "Tie him down so he doesn't hit the overhead when we go irrational, much as I'm tempted."

Two of the officers chained him down to the captain's chair, activating the grav restraints. Captain Rican doubted they were going to really go irrational, the Girati word for N-space calculation, but he probably meant when the system went offline and gravity failed on bounce. When up and down became matters of preference. It was the security officer, it seemed, the King of hearts, who spoke.

"Pix says we have attitude and thrusters. Main engine will take a moment, core was in shutdown when we got here. She's inverted and heavy, just keep that in mind."

He paged through the screens with an ease of a ship-born. "We're gonna have to roll her..."

"Actually, sir, with our current speed that's a bad idea. I suggest that we just slingshot, she's too fast to spin without a chance of altering our course." That was the Greek god seated at the con. He tapped a few more buttons. "I'd be able to do it, but it'd be hard and no promise we don't ding her up."

The grim reaper nodded. "Then take her down and under, bring her up hot and plot to miss the nav-sat on the far side."

"Aye sir."

The order was given, and they went about carrying it out without more than a few phrases in whatever language they spoke amongst themselves.

"All right, Grab steel. Ri, Give us a Ten count, please." Reaper moved, for the first time, closer to the door, where he could lean over and grab a handhold. Gravity science was still new, and most people knew the gravity drills in case of failure, but truth was, on a ship, it was rare... But these people moved to their places as if they did this all the time.

One, the king of hearts, coming to check the captain over and make sure he didn't have any poison or weapons capable of doing himself in. He also took a moment to strip him of his insignia and rank pins.

"Captain Rican, you are found to be in violation of International space Convention 25, willful defiance of Earth Authority and solar governance, you have been stripped of your rank, and your ship has been confiscated by the New Government. You are assured a trial, fair and impartial but we must remind you that anything you say will be used against you, and any violence against our persons or this ship, will be met with equal force. You will have right to counsel, and it will be provided upon landing. Do you understand these rights?"

As much as the captain wanted to say 'get bent,' which he knew in more than one language, he knew these guys were serious,

"I understand, I invoke my right to remain silent."

The king of hearts nodded and tightened the straps. While uncomfortable, he wasn't being mean; he didn't know how hard the bounce would be or how bad the gee force was. "See that you do."

There was ice in the sentence. Seconds seemed to take hours. It was less than a minute; he knew that, but is seemed like ten years later when the Greek god spoke again. But first, he tapped on the bulkhead as if to get attention, a sign which Captain

Rican later learned meant 'mark' The entire bridge fell silent as the singular voice started counting the seconds. And with each word, those who were around were making last preparations, stowing the dead, and strapping in or grabbing a handhold, or in the current vernacular 'grabbing steel.'

"Desh"

"En'a" Ri said, not even bothering to translate. He was speaking for his people so that everyone was on the same timer. He didn't care if the captain could understand him.

The countdown paused a moment as he spoke in Standard again. "Pix I need more power or we'll auger in."

"Copy," said the small voice from the other conn. "I'm having trouble with the engineering feed, we're still not at full power."

"Ri" as he had been called, grunted and punched a sequence on his own screen before reaching over and hitting a button on the screen next to him where the other conn officer sat. A moment later, the problem seemed to be fixed as the steel began to shimmy and the lights to change as the heat rose.

"Oxto,"

"Efta..." He tapped a few more buttons. "Clear of all pods, we have a bounce course set."

"Course charted away from debris." Helm replied. "She's a little sluggish so time it early or we'll be too late, we gotta hit pretty steep or we won't have room to burn off this speed before we hit titan.

Orion seemed unfazed, his voice was even, still counting. What language, the captain didn't know, but the countdown was still going; about the half-way point if the captain had kept up.

"Shov,"

"Panj"

"Shtar."

The cadence never varied. There was never more or less pause between the words, as if he were watching a timer tick down. He grabbed a hold of one of the handholds.

"Gravity critical, grab steel."

The effect was eerie. A single voice never varying in pitch or cadence, counting down, curt commands given in the same matter-of-fact voice that never varied in tone.

And still, the countdown continued. There was no more urgency in the words, no sign that the count was ending except the silent preparations that the others were making.

"Trin,"

"Duy"

"Yek,"

"Impact." There was silence for a moment, and the captain thought maybe the count was wrong, but then he remembered them saying they'd time it early, which meant it was taking a moment to catch up. Then he felt the ship begin to move.

The whole ship shook and shimmied as they fought to get her out of the dive. Fighting gravity was a matter of pitch and all they could do at the moment was skim the atmosphere down and back up until they could use the speed to catapult out of the atmosphere and away from Terra. It was all just a matter of keeping her steady and on course. A few more panels sparked, and the captain was treated to what he figured were curse words, but being they were neither Girati nor Standard, he was left to guess at the colorful language.

Time seemed to slow again as the entire team seemed to hold their breaths, most holding their handhold, a few clutching for dear life, were uncomfortable with gravity maneuvers. The shaking didn't just stop; it stopped with the suddenness and ferocity of an impact. Everyone was thrown into their harness or away from the floor as the stressed gravity system failed, unable to compensate both for the gravity and the intense heat as it shuttled power to critical shielding to protect the computers. After the shaking stopped, there was nothing but null g for almost forty seconds.

"Gravity coming down, Grab steel." The two most dangerous times were when the gravity stopped, it could send you flying, and when it restarted. These guys were Girati trained, and it showed, they had an arm around the handhold and were still working, some only held by a leg around a hold. They were used to null.

The lights came back up to normal, the red cast gone, and the ship wasn't shimmying anymore. "We are free of Terra's gravity, engines shut down, thrusters active." The Greek god said.

"And we missed the satellite." It seemed to be some sort of inside joke between them as the Grim Reaper smiled. He let go of the handhold, and the captain marveled. The hologram didn't so much as flicker. Reaper turned to the Greek God.

"Figure out where this thing will end up and send the signal to blackbird."

"Signal sent, ping started. Retrieval crew en route. Rendezvous in ten. Let's get the captain packaged."

They didn't use mag restraints, something that surprised the captain, but they did use shackles, old school, actual chain, they said they found them harder for people to deal with because they were heavy and couldn't be overwritten. He had to hand it to them. They were good.

When the crew came over, they handed the ship over, but the captain came with them. He was loaded into blackbird, which turned out to be an old Anari Jump ship. Or at least that was what he thought it was. He was seated, arms tied to the rail about head height.

"Might want to grab steel," the pilot said.

There wasn't just the hand-hold above him to which his arms were tied, but also a T bar near his ankles he could slide his legs under to keep himself from being propelled up and breaking his arm or his neck as he flipped over. Fortunately the captain had the good sense to listen because when the main drive kicked in it took them from idle to near-irrational in seconds, leaving no choice but to turn off the gravity or have human jam instead of passengers. When the jumpship stopped, dropping from FTL, gravity didn't come back slowly, but all at once with a violence that took his breath away.

Some of the Avengers had taken their holo's off, but not Reaper, he still stood, stoically un-moved, hand near, what the captain assumed was a knife, seeming to read a book and keep an eye on the captain at the same time.

A few minutes after gravity came back, they docked, and captain Rican found himself being transferred to the same high security prison into which his namesake had vanished over a decade before. And he would make them regret it. That was his one promise. If it was the last thing he did.

A New Mandate

The IRT had done their job and done it well. The ship was back in space dock and other than the damage already done, there was little else. A few small hull breaches sealed with Insti-seal that needed to be properly looked at. But now the conversation turned to what to do with her. The ship was huge, the biggest of the fleet, and beautiful, even if her legacy was ugly. She'd been commissioned twelve years ago after the capture of Admiral Ithica Rican. A man so hated and feared that much of the talk now centered on destroying his namesake, the ship they had just spent time and money to rescue. Besides the fact that they couldn't chance it coming down within population centers, the impact with the atmosphere could have had serious lasting impacts to the already destroyed ecology.

Finally, one of the admirals stood. Admiral Akani Jensen, half-Alcarin, but gifted with his mother's features and longevity, and his Girati Father's strong sense of right and wrong, he couldn't just sit and listen. He was immediately recognized. He spoke directly to the Chancellor pro tempore. The Chancellor Pro Tempore was the leader until they got their elections. They didn't want to rush it and chance foul play, or loaded ballots and things like that. The chancellor was on the Ballot too, and he hoped he'd be able to bring the world back to what it should be. The chancellor was a Lunar.

From the single colony on Luna, his father had worked the shipyard, his mother worked hospitality, helping care for the captains that stayed while they cared for the ships.

"Sir, I know you are all for slagging the ship, but we have gone to so much trouble to save it, it seems like a shame, and furthermore, it's a waste of resources and manpower we don't have. If she is slagged, it will take us three years to create another flagship. But, my project can have her back to flying condition in a year. Back on the line within eighteen months. Half the time, a third the cost, and with a boost in moral that we sorely need."

He paused, stepping forward so his friend could better see him.

The chancellor nodded. That was something to consider. "It is no secret that we battle with the monster that is morale. There are many who say we will do no better than those we replace, that we will do worse, that we will not care about the people we are supposed to protect. And slagging this ship, even with her past, would prove that." He acknowledged.

"She was the last ship created at Luna Shipyards, and if we slag her, we may never be able to get the shipyards back. But with my plan, we use the workers from the shipyard that created her, retrofit her, get rid of any trace of OSU, give them back their livelihood and maybe, just maybe, be able to actually get the shipyards running again."

He wasn't really playing dirty, but he did know that the Chancellor pro Tempore had been raised on Luna. He knew how much the shipyard meant to them. It was the primary source of income, and two of the three bays had been utterly destroyed by orbital bombardment.

"Eighteen months?" The chancellor said.

"Yes sir. And we have enough resources from some of the other destroyed ships that can be clean-processed back into useable base materials for fixing this ship, thus cutting costs still farther. And, we would again have a proud heritage behind our ship, but it would not dripping in the blood of the innocent but rather with the sweat of the hardworking people working for a brighter future."

Now it was time to bring his argument home. "Sir, we both know, Lunars are a proud people, and they won't take handouts, but they will take a contract and it will bring money to the colonists, money that will be used to stabilize the economy, and with the repair contract on the newly named ship, they will have a reason to repair the yards, and can be certain we haven't forgotten them."

That was their biggest fear, to be forgotten on the singular outpost on Luna. The sprawling underground city and the shipyard were on the dark side of the moon. They always worried about being forgotten by their cousins. They were an island totally dependent on outsiders for everything, but everything they gave was well worth the cost. They were one of the few who didn't always take credits. Instead, they took whatever could be used or traded. A lot of people joking called them "Planetary Girati" because they had the same sort of sense of right and wrong, and they were some of the best traders in the galaxy. To be called a Lunar was a mark of pride.

"I agree." The chancellor said. "And I believe you are the man for the job since you spoke so well for it. But I caution you there are still many people who want to see that ship fail, see it destroyed, and with it the hope of our small government. The fate of this government may rest on this ship and its crew."

"Thank you sir, I will be mindful." It wasn't unexpected. No one else was speaking to save the ship, so there was no surprise it was assigned to him. Hopefully, by the time the ship was ready and space worthy with a crew, the election would be over and they would have a president who wouldn't take them into the dark ages again, or he could foresee a repeat of recent history and the advent of another bloody war from which theymight never emerge.

The Decision

Admiral Jensen ran his hand through his white hair. His eyes were amethyst and blinked tiredly as he stared at the nameless hulk of dura-steel alloy and rivets that writhed and pulsed under the onslaught of the repair crews that worked on her.

Devoid of a name, she was only known by the date the order was given to strip her of the name the OSU had given her. It had been months; the ship was now mostly ready, a few weeks from being able to hold atmosphere, and so now, he had to deal with commissioning a crew. In a perfect world, he knew who he wanted, but the person he wanted had another job. Of course, he knew who realistically he wanted. Unfortunately, because it had been his idea, he'd been told that he would be responsible for it. And now, he was left with decisions like this.

Who to put in the captain's chair? It was clear that it had to be someone of "uncommon valor" as the saying used to be, a man of strong mettle and stronger sense of right and wrong.

All of which this man was. But was that enough? And with what he'd been through, was there enough left in him to give that level of devotion to the crew and the ship? He'd seen Girati

Captains burnout, and that was the last thing he wanted for his friend. But as angry as he'd be for asking the question, it had to be asked.

Was there enough of him left, enough heart and soul to deal with the rigors of a crew? The last he'd heard, the old man was drinking and brawling. Trying to get away from the memory of the family and crew he had lost. That was a bad place for anyone, but worse for a Girati captain.

It'd been nearly two days that he'd been wrestling with the list of names, at first it had been forty, but some of them had not made the security sweep, a couple were dead, one had retired and returned home and one was at Valley of the Stars. That left him with twelve names.

The admiral turned back to the files spread out in uneven lines on his desk. One sitting by itself in the corner. He knew who he wanted, but he had to make sure that this wasn't prejudice, as his friend. That he really was the best man for the job. And he had to be certain there was anything left of the man he'd known. That question had to be answered first. So he'd pulled the file, still hard-copy, like everything else they trusted. And he'd browsed it.

He wasn't sure where his friend was right now, hopefully out in the rim making trouble, but knowing him, probably not. They'd lost track of him, but he was either in one of the canteens getting drunk and brawling, or he was in jail. Neither option looked good for him.

The friend in question was Tyrell Hansen. Or simply, Tyrell. Like many Girati, he didn't go by his house name. Just his common name. The government hated Tyrell; he was a wild card to most of them.

Tyrell was over two hundred, but looked between twenty-five and thirty, depending on how tired he was. Tyrell was a Girati Free Singer, not bound to ship and stone like most of them. He could stay on a Girati ship, but didn't have to. And he hadn't set foot on 'free' steel that bore a stone since his ship had been badly damaged in a raid a little more than a decade before. The raid that had nearly destroyed him.

For his many shortcomings, there was one thing that no one would argue about if they knew him. Tyrell was a force of nature in the chair. He demanded loyalty and respect and got it even from the most hardened crews. They had seen him whip any bunch of misfits into shape with a bit of mutual respect and a lot of grifter grit. He didn't take nothing from no one. And they knew it. They could say whatever they wanted, but Tyrell was something special.

Unfortunately, his Girati sensibilities often overrode his common sense, and that was why he'd been promoted on the battlefield four times, it was also why he'd been busted down five times. He wouldn't, couldn't put up with injustice or mistreatment, and he would balk long and loud if anyone tried, and hang the consequences.

The Admiral put down his friend's folder, noting with dismay that it was thicker than it had been the last time he pulled it, full of new arrests and quarrels started for good cause. And he started going through the other files. Quickly the twelve names went to four, when he pulled any that didn't have deep space experience. Two more went when he found out they didn't deal with aliens well. Xenophobia was a luxury they didn't have. And that left two names.

Tyrell and another man named John Hooper. There was something about that name that stuck in the back of the Admiral's mind and he quickly made a decision. He called for a courier. The young man who came in wore the black drab of a unit. His eyes were covered with a navigation visor, and his face was blank. The threads could be seen where a patch had been ripped off his tunic, one that had been there for a very long time. If you looked closely you could still read the faint imprint of numbers and letters. But the Admiral didn't look closely, he didn't want to know. Not because the boy was a unit, but because he couldn't afford to get pulled into a black project before the ship launched. As long as she was in space, it would be harder to destroy her.

Knowing that, he handed the young man the requisition order. He was pretty sure what he was going to find when he read the documents on Mr. Hooper. Plea without Elocution, he never said what he did, or even that what he did was wrong, just took a plea deal because he was 'just following orders' a theory that held water like a sieve.

"Take this to the file room, and bring the records back hard-copy." He said, handing over the documents. "And take this to the postmaster and have quarters requisitioned for Tyrell."

"Yes sir." The young man's face was blank behind the visor that hid his eyes. "Anything else?"

"No, that's all."

"Permission to speak?" He still stood ramrod straight. Not even daring to make eye contact, though the visor hid his eyes.

"Go ahead."

"Do--" He was quiet. "Do you know where I can buy peaches?" The admiral stopped to process that for a moment. He had both tipped his hand and kept himself from getting in trouble at the same time.

"I don't know if they are in season, but if you check back with me I can give you the name of a vendor." He smiled, hoping the young man understood that he did know how to free him, but needed time to get it done.

"I was hoping to get some for my sister's memorial. She liked them so much, and I wanted to try and bake a pie."

"Of course, I'll see if I can find some."

"Thank you, sir." The young man walked off, his face still blank, but his eyes shining and his resolve strengthened. But his eyes, covered by the visor, were also slightly purple, there were only two beings in the galaxy with purple eyes, the first were the Alcarins, but the boy had no Alcarin features, and the eyes would have been the wrong color. The second was the Girati, but purple eyes were a sign of something horribly, frighteningly wrong, they were the sign of a stone gone rogue.

Cult of N4m31355

The few OSU, or Patrol people who would talk about the place, and there were never many who would, called the place "The field of the Forgotten" and they tried to forget it. There was a very simple reason no one talked to outsiders. N4M31355. She didn't like them talking to outsiders. They didn't even joke that she was a child anymore.

They didn't even know what to call her. Human, obviously not. So, when they had to, they called her "nameless." And they hid the fact that it was a person under the numbers and letters of their project name N4M31355. If you looked at it it bore the hint of the word Nameless. But those who watched her, or it, never listened to her. In fact, it was the first rule of working here. Pacify her, keep her calm but don't engage her in conversation, that way lay madness.

She talked in pictures and half-stories, the ramblings of a girl who had lost her mind. So far, she didn't attack anyone wearing her name. But for the rest of them... John turned away. He couldn't watch her consume another human. He'd tried to stop her once, and in return he got the powers that were slowly killing him. He had known her once, a long time ago, under a different name. A human one, one he barely dared to think. He tried to tally up how long it had been, but his mind balked at what his computer told him. He should have been dead and dust long ago, but she had spared him, at least that was what she said. In his mind it was torture.

He'd been John for so long he didn't know if he remembered his first name. But when they had found him, it was in an escape pod, a sliver of purple driven into his chest. It should have killed him but didn't. The doctors said they couldn't remove the shard. They called it a miracle that he was alive. But his memories, they only came back in pieces, and even then, mostly only when he slept. The last time he had been able to remember, he had tried to kill her, but even that was beyond him now. He could feel the memories slipping again and he turned to see what even he was too terrified to speak of.

He looked over the field of statues and looked to the now-quiet obelisk. He wanted to stop it, but he didn't know how and no one here would help him. So few of them understood what she was. Where they were, what this place used to be. None of them knew what question to ask or to answer. He had once, but now, so long ago, he had forgotten.

His hand ran over the panel he had long since lost the ability to see. His hands found the buttons by rote. But they hesitated for a moment. Could he really share that abomination with anyone? Could he? But he had to. He had to call for help. But the system on the ship was old, unimaginably old. Old beyond the human measure of years. And for all those years, he had listened to her whisper. Long ago, he had wanted to use what they all carried, but she had batted it out of his hand when she could still move. Broken the vial, and he had had fits for weeks just from the vapors of the poison.

It had taken his sight and her ability to totally control him, but it hadn't been enough to kill him. He doubted there was much left that could. And he regretted all that he had brought to her. Those, he had simply handed a crystal and told to wait in the statuary. Few of them ever made it far enough to see the guardians, and the few who did never left unchanged. Some never left at all. More toys for her collection.

He didn't feel the statue move. He'd long forgotten that they could. He was so used to it. He'd forgotten a lot of things. Her name, the name of the steel under his feet, what fresh non-canned air felt like, and most of all he'd forgotten his own name.

He did remember a few things. He remembered that she was deadly. He remembered that once, long ago, she'd been a girl, and he remembered her birthday.

He'd decided today, on what would have been her birthday, today was the day he would ask for help. Today, he would tell the universe of the crime that led to this. He knew he wasn't likely to live long enough to see the help that arrived, but he certainly wasn't expecting to almost not have enough time to send it.

"Please, come quickly." He thought as the world went black around him and his blood stained the purple crystal of the knife. As his body cooled, he became stone, bright red crystal where his blood once was, and solid, immoveable stone for the rest of eternity. But the signal had been sent. And he had no way of knowing what that signal would do.

On the wall, a timer set for eight minutes. The Commander wasn't sure what it was about, but he watched, the young Unit had been given a reprimand and things changed, and the timer clicked on but didn't start to count yet. The young man stiffened, eyes going dark purple. Not a common thing.

While it was common for a Unit's eyes to glow, purple was not a common color. Purple was a bad color, and with the information retained, he went abruptly offline sliding into a deep sleep that even a Reprimand couldn't wake him from. A few minutes went by, and he opened his eyes. They were glowing deep purple, and he now stood straight as if the restraints didn't bother him at all.

7:00

"What is your name?"

"We are the nameless." Purple eyes stared back at the doctor. "We are the nameless and the forgotten."

"Well, he didn't give himself a name," the doctor said. But this was still off script, and now even the reprimands seemed to have no effect.

"We are the nameless, and the forgotten will come, back from nowhere, they come, and all the dead come with them. Memory, and forgetting, and song and cold and silence, you have splintered it, you don't know what you have done, but one is chosen, one will help us, he will take us, and we will destroy her."

His voice wasn't monotone, it almost sounded like he was speaking with more than one voice. Speaking with a voice of many. "The named among the nameless will kill her."

"Who?"

"Nameless."

6:00

"This happened the last time he was reprimanded?" The doctor asked as he watched the young man stare off into nothing. If he was a normal Unit, he would say he was updating.

He nodded. "Every time he gets a class two reprimand. "We can't find a carrier signal either." The tech said. "It's always like this but the words change a little. This is the first time he's been so vocal though. Usually it's a lot of staring."

"Cancel the reprimand code, if it's not doing any good let's not waste it."

The tech nodded. "Once he gets into this altered state there isn't much we can do, but the last time we talked about our options, even behind closed doors, he threw one of our techs into the wall." The tech frowned. "Broke bones he tossed him so hard, didn't even touch him. He has a hundred times the strength of a regular unit and is psionic to boot. It appears we have run into some old programming, and we can't control him. The reprimands stop working and his pain receptors are blocked, as long as his eyes stay purple. We've never had the whole thing last more than eight minutes." He nodded to the time clock. "That's why we time it."

4:00

The young man moved his arms, and the bands dropped off him as if they were nothing. They knew better than to apologize, but he showed no anger. There was nearly a minute of silence before the young man moved or spoke again. He walked over to the picture window, which the doctor nodded for the tech to Unfrost, as a Unit wouldn't trigger the protocol. Bright purple eyes locked on the ship, and he placed his hand on the window. "That is the ship." He turned back to the doctor for a moment. "Who flies that Ship?"

"No one." The doctor was pretty sure there was no crew right now. The Unit looked back at the ship and then the doctor.

"I want to meet No one." He smiled. "I must meet no one, that's the ship she wants, that's the ship she will take. I must meet No one. I must tell him." He frowned as if receiving a reprimand, but the computer system was flat. "I must warn No one, that the nameless wants the ship without a name. But as long as it holds no name, she has no way to take it."

0:05

"She comes, I must go."

A moment later, the fit ended, and he lay as a man nearly dead. "In about two minutes he will have no memory of what he said or did." The doctor looked at the ship.

"See what we can find about that ship, maybe we can find a way to slip some Units on board."

"Its part of the new Government sir. I'll see what I can do, but they refuse to abide by the code."

Called Up

Tyrell was used to this, the march down the corridor at a pace that was often barely too fast, so the Patrol officer was mostly carrying him. This young man, though his stride was efficient, didn't walk faster than the partially sober man could follow, and the hand on his arm was perfunctory, no real pressure behind it. Of course, it didn't help that Tyrell was drunk. Not just a little, a lot drunk, falling down, sleep it off, drunk. Only the fact that the guards had run him headfirst into the field managed to wake him up a bit.

Tyrell only brawled when he was drunk, because it was only then that his Girati sensibilities would override his common sense, but they had insulted his daughter and her steel, on this, the anniversary of her passing.

It had been enough to set him off. Tyrell looked around blearily. It had been a two-day ride and the alcohol still had left him fuzzy. He must have been more drunk than he remembered.

The sensation of shackled hands came back to him and he realized that he was in restraints and being walked down a hallway that looked vaguely familiar, but he didn't know why. And the shoulder patch of the Unit officer leading him was Ground Patrol.

As far as Patrol officers, this one was being polite. The only thing Tyrell knew about this kid was that he was known by the patrol as K101. And he looked very young, probably no older than most humans would judge him to be, so early twenties, maybe. Probably conscripted during his year of service.

The young man stopped at the requisitioned quarters and passed a hand over the scan pad, only to have it beep at him. He sighed and undid the restraints on the prisoner. A word and a pass of his hands and the arms were unlocked from the chest plate, which was slid over Tyrell's head. Then a touch of the shackles and they came off in his hand. They were coded to the DNA of certain people. Anyone else tried that and they would cinch tighter.

The young Unit slipped the chest plate back in the carrier along with the shackles before turning to the door. He gestured with a flat hand.

"These are your quarters, you do have free run of the station, but you have been asked to refrain from leaving the station without checking in or without escort, failure to do so may result in your re-arrest. The young man spoke flatly, with the inflection of rote. Only the flat-hand gesture said that he had once been kin.

Normally Tyrell found himself thrust into quarters unceremoniously, which meant whoever had paid the bill was powerful. He didn't know that his benefactor was one of his oldest friends and one of the rear admirals of the fleet.

The Admiral had ended up paying not only his bail, but the damages fine to have him released without trial or jail time. And, of course, the OSU wanted to keep an eye on him so he wouldn't get in any more trouble, or more likely hoped he did so they could get more money from his benefactor.

They had no idea that Tyrell was being tapped by the new government, and if they had, they would have kept him in jail indefinitely. Tyrell placed his hand on the door scanner and the doors opened. The lights went to spacer normal; the gravity snapping to the 2/3 that space-born preferred. The change in gravity made him stumble for a moment, too used to the firm Terran Gravity that he had been stuck with recently, and too close to drunk to compensate immediately. It also told him that this person knew not only that he was Girati, but that he was space-born. That narrowed the list considerably.

"What's your name kid?" he said as he righted himself and gestured for the young man to come in. Since he had been asked, albeit not verbally, he was allowed.

"I am called K-101." He said quietly, with the practiced flatness in his voice. Units did whatever they could to make themselves sound non-human. It was part of how they were schooled.

"That's a designation not a name." Tyrell shook his head. "What name did your parents give you?"

"My kind don't get a name sir." His arms were unnaturally stiff at his side, but his voice couldn't quite get back to that mindless monotone they were known for. That question had jolted him. Most people paid no mind to Units. They were part of the wall or furniture.

"We have no names," the young man repeated helplessly, trying to return to script. Tyrell smiled and said what he knew the boy wanted to say and couldn't.

"Bullshit," he said. "All people have a name, and I bet you had one before you became patrol."

"I did, but it is forbidden from me." he said, his voice cracking slightly. "We are allowed to see what they want us to see, and say what words they give us, sir."

"You know that isn't the way it is supposed to be." The young man was silent a long moment before he answered.

"I know it is the way it is, sir. And beyond that I have no opinion on the matter." He returned to the script, his voice flat again as he found himself back in territory he knew how to deal with. There was a long moment of silence. "I don't have a name, but I am not one of the Nameless." He blinked and returned to himself. "I'm sorry, please disregard whatever was said, my program is glitching."

Tyrell was going to confront him about it, but that would only bring the young man pain as the system they had wired into him sent reprimands to keep him on script. In fact, he thought, that might be the reason for the altered state, too many reprimands, a Unit that wanted to be free. Tyrell changed tactics. "What is your opinion on peaches?"

"I love them, sir." He said with a smile. Knowing the double-meaning behind the word.

Tyrell understood. The boy was forced to say what he said. "Maybe they can get you assigned to my ship." He said, thinking of his Girati steel. "We have lots of peaches."

Girati ships were called 'free steel " for a reason. "Free steel" meant any sort of prisoner was free. Unit, slave, it didn't matter. They were free as long as they were on free steel.

"Maybe, sir, I have a month or two before my current contract is up."

"You are dismissed K-101, I will not keep you from your duties."

"Thank you, sir." With that he turned to leave. Tyrell turned to see the picture window, the entire bulkhead on one side, unfrost to reveal the ship in the bay. This, then, was the repair station. The young man's inability to enter then was because hallways were common, but rooms were private, so unless he was asked to enter, he couldn't.

"Computer," he said, with the clipped tone this computer understood. "What ship is that in the bay?"

"That ship has no name." The computer said without elaboration.

"Explain."

"The ship has been stripped of its name and designation number; it was created at Luna Shipyards twelve years ago, and was nearly destroyed in the war. It is now being retrofitted to meet USL specifications, and will be renamed and crewed," the computer said simply.

Ambushed

"Call in Tyrell." The rear-admiral said to the young officer in the hallway. It was always better to ambush than to ask with him. So everything was ready when the young man came in. The man still looked young, thirties, no swagger like most captains, and he seemed— pulled in, as if expecting the gravity to go off any second. His hair was dark, his eyes were coffee brown, and his words, despite all the training, still bore the lilt of a spacer. And around his neck was a red Girati crystal.

"Raise your right hand."

Tyrell was used to being ambushed. He'd been promoted on the battlefield twice, so he knew the drill. But this was slightly different.

"I, state your name," The Admiral said, officially.

"I, Tyrell John Syracuse Newton-Hansen," he replied, using his full name for the first time in nearly ten years.

"Do solemnly swear to faithfully discharge the duties of the rank of Captain, in the USL fleet."

"Do solemnly swear to faithfully discharge the duties of the rank of Captain in the USL fleet." He said, his voice pausing as he realized what oath he was being given. He was a captain again.

"Keep your hand up." The admiral said. "Among these duties, are to secure, crew and captain the steel that once bore the name of the Rican." He used the Girati word for ship because it had no name. "If you intend to do this with all faith, and to the best of your ability, then signify by saying 'aye'"

"Aye," he said. It took a moment for his brain to catch up. He wasn't just a captain, he was a captain of his own steel. It might be USL steel but his own to captain none-the-less.

"I know it isn't the way we normally do it, but this ship at the moment doesn't have a name, a command crew, or most of her outer hull. We can re-do this later if you feel the need, but as far as I'm concerned you are dully noted as the captain of the vessel. USLS 2019, with your commission active immediately, I need you to get her flying again. I can get you anyone you need."

"Why the urgency?"

"We are trying to get her flight worthy before the insurgents can blow her out of the sky. She was the last ship made at Luna Shipyards, and she will be the last until we can get them repaired, but I can't bear the thought of a ship like that being mothballed or slagged. She's slated for n-space needles, so we need to get her space worthy to get her out to the Yard where they can be installed."

"And then?"

"Her mission is to connect with any other inhabited worlds that can be found. Treaty and trade. There are a lot of human descendants out there that may look different from us, but they deserve to know that the war that drove them away is over."

"Alcaris?"

"If you feel you need to, and if you can get there without endangering yourself or the planet. I know they are not fans of humans."

"Thank you, sir."

"Requisition yourself a proper uniform; it will be at least a week before the shell is habitable. Your quarters are yours until your ship is underway."

"Thank you, sir."

"Don't thank me yet. It is going to be a lot harder this time, you are going to the rift and beyond. So whatever prayers and obligations you have to say, do it. And you're going to be using N-space. Not to mention some of your crew will be aliens."

"And I have to promote harmony."

"And all that human bullshit." The Admiral smiled, throwing his oft-repeated words back at him. "But if any man can do the job, you can." He patted his old friend on the shoulder and turned back to watch the ship. "You're dismissed."

Tyrell had gotten back to his quarters, laid down, suddenly tired, and as he drifted off, he tasted chemicals, and thought, for a moment he saw a man in his peripheral vision. But before he could do anything, a cold darkness took him and he knew nothing.

"Why do they fall?" The voice was that of a child. Maybe eight or nine. A familiar voice, but one so long removed from his history he couldn't put a name or a face to it. "Why do they fall and leave me alone?" She was a girl, dark-haired, he wasn't sure of her eye color, but she wore a sliver of crystal around her neck, but unlike his own, which was red, with a few black streaks caused by the death of his wife, hers was a beautiful rich purple.

That frightened him, but at that exact moment, he wasn't sure why. Purple Girati crystal was so rare it wasn't much more than a legend.

She pouted, playing with the crystal. "I brought them pretty crystals but they wouldn't play with them. I sang for them but they covered their ears. I danced for them but no one joined me. And then they all fell."

Her voice was sad. "Or worse yet they disappeared. They all said they would be back, but nothing I do, no asking or cajoling, will bring them back. Where did they go?"

He felt a tug on his sleeve in the dream. As he turned, the ship filled itself in around him, but only as far as he could see, and only at the height of the little girl. "Why did you leave me Ty-ty?"

His brain spun, trying to find a name for that person, the one who was so familiar with him as to use a name that only a few even knew. It didn't occur to him that this was a dream, and that in a dream people know things they shouldn't know. But his mind tried uselessly to pull up a scrap of information about the one who would be able to use that name.

"I had to; the song made me leave."

"Then I will sing a new song, louder than the one that drove you 'way and I will bring you back. You can stay with me."

"I may not be able to stay."

"I will make the song keep you, and I will put you away where I can find you, so I won't be alone."

"You know you can't do that."

"I can."

"You shouldn't. Ona does not like it when we force others to do something."

"But I'm tired of being alone, and they all go away, they all fall. They don't even remember my name. Do you?"

"You're..." The name died before he could say it. There was nothing but dead, nothing but the dim wail of the dead and the song of the stone as it walked. The voice went from angry to sad and lost, "I don't remember my name either. But no one will come to me, no one will dance with me, no one will sing with me. They all just whisper. And no one will tell me my name."

"They whisper about me in corridors, 'nameless' they call me. But no one comes to visit."

Tyrell woke up, trying to remember the girl's name, and feeling like she was someone he really knew. And it bothered him. Why couldn't he remember her name? If she was a child, then he had to have known her recently.

"But," his brain said. "You haven't been called Ty-ty by a child since before your wife died."

That put it at least ten years ago. She wouldn't be a child anymore. And she didn't feel like a child, more like the faded memory of a child. As if that was all she could remember... or all she had ever learned.

But there really wasn't anything else he could do. He had no way of knowing how long ago he'd known her and the records of the past hundred years were spotty at best.

He stopped to think about it, trying to remember how old he was. He'd been out on the rim a good long while, and it wasn't uncommon out there to lose time. Near as he could tell by memory and current date, he'd been born about two hundred and twelve years ago. And he didn't look a day over thirty.

Captain's Log

CAPTAIN'S LOG, GAILBRAITH STATION.

My ship sits out there just beyond the frosted glass, and it gleams so differently than the ship that I am used to, but its sleeker, an A frame ship, she looks like the rays you sometimes see in the history vids of Pre-War Terra. This is the first time I have been within a hundred light years of Terra, the first world of my own volition, in generations.

My friend has called upon me to captain a ship. He knows I have lost my steel, that all my kin are dead, and still, he puts this on me. But somehow, I think he knows, he understands, I am not alive without a ship; I am simply pretending to live.

I don't like our mission much, more of the shake-hands Klitspa that we have to do, go out and see who still remembers terra. But somewhere out there, there are Girati Ships from the time before, and many others, others we have only begun to meet, Tucuran ships, and Alcarins, and many others.

This is a mixed cruise, no Moiety, which was something I had to get used to. Though on a Girati ship its less to protect the women from the men, than to protect the men from the women, an angry Girati woman is something to behold.

I don't know how I feel about not having a name for the ship, but maybe she will tell me. I checked the records, and such a thing has been done among the Girati in times of need or war, so it's not unheard of. It's not taboo. But a ship without a stone, another thing to get used to. But she has her own sort of music.

I'm sitting here, looking over files, and trying to figure out not just who is best for the ship, but who is best for our mission. I refuse to let us be like all the other ships, I refuse to paint the xenophobic picture of the patrols, I want there to be no mistake when we hail them that we are from this particular ship, whatever name we end up with.

My first choice for security is, of all things, a Wraith. But I have found her record exemplary, and her work ethic beyond reproach. I also find that, she is personable if you are personable, but they have said she is having trouble adjusting, but I read that as people are having trouble dealing with having a Wraith on the station.

She turned me down, but I plan to see her today, bring her the clearance pass to get on the ship. It expires as soon as we launch, but I hope bringing it proves to her that I'm serious and not just playing with her.

My pilot is an old friend, a spacer. He took his Aja with me. Half Girati, half Resan, he's an odd one, elfin features with Girati stature and blond hair.

My doctor's half-Tucuran, Comes highly recommended. And of all people I got Magic to run engineering, Som'a'son is Denvalian but his wife was a friend of my wife. And so we've passed word on occasion.

But of all of them, the one I don't want to talk to the most is AJ. I love him like a brother; I don't want to tell him that my daughter, his wife, the mistress of the ship, is dead, and almost all the crew with her.

Security

Tyrell's breath fogged and hung as he entered the room. The room was cold. Very cold, but Tyrell— no, the captain, expected that. He was still getting used to lots of things, calling himself Captain again, the new uniforms, better than some, but still uncomfortable, and the reception he was getting at the station. That took getting used to. But right now, he was visiting the person he hoped to be his chief of security. She was a first in a lot of ways. First person besides himself, assigned to the crew, First woman on the crew, first Wraith on a long-space voyage with a valid commission. That was if he could get her to accept. Which was why he was here, freezing his li-yang off and making himself an open target. He knew better than to bring a weapon into a cold source room.

The quarters were also dark. He'd knocked, but there had been no response. Though, the Wraith were not known for knocking. He tried not to strain to see her. Jenna, he'd heard a lot about her. Most of it he knew was J'gash, the slime you wiped off your shoes on marshy worlds. Lower than trash. He had heard that she was reclusive, and he had hoped it was due to her difficulty with socializing, but he knew it was more likely because humans were afraid of her.

He clicked his best approximation of a greeting. And was surprised to hear a trill just in front of him as the lights came up to a dimness somewhere between cloudy day and twilight.

"What are you doing here, hot-source?"

Humans and Wraith had been in a sort of luke-warm war for ages. Neither one survived very well on the others' territory so the war was in fits and starts. And both sides blamed the other. In reality it was both. A bunch of miscommunications coupled with the human penchant for taking what is not theirs and trying to make everything theirs, and the disregard for the lives of the Wraith, the Programmers, and everyone else on the cold grid, had started the war. Wraith were seen as a threat. He thought they were pretty, in a sort of frightening way. And they were the best beings in the universe when it came to computers and multi-dimensional geometry.

But most of all, they were good at exactly what he needed her for: security. Wraith were good with computers, even Human Computers, and she had the benefit of being able to stand vacuum for short periods of time, so if they ever needed it, she could sneak in without restarting atmo. But the figure that met his eyes was wearing a visored helmet.

"Can I help you-- Captain?" The last word was curious. She'd never had a captain come looking for her. Especially after she said no.

"You won't need that." He pointed to the helmet. "When I hire crew, I want them to show who they really are. No masks, no games."

Slowly, a silver-gray hand wrapped in wires reached up to pull off the helmet. The face underneath was white, the eyes used to be brown, now turned more red by the nanobots in her system. One eye was prosthetic, her socket turned to the gray-black metal so many knew and feared. Her hair fell in wires, coils and braids down to her hips and clicked against the hard carapace that covered her legs in wires and metal. One hand was still human, white but marked with wires, the nails rendered in the odd-hematite metal that was the first stage of conversion.

He smiled at her and clicked affirmative. Before approaching slowly. "I came to prove what I said," he said quietly. "I appreciate seeing your true face, not some--stand-in." He had to think of the standard word they used. He was careful not to stare, but he was also careful not to flinch or pull away. Though he was tempted to stare because he considered her strikingly beautiful in a deadly sort of way.

"You came to me, hot-source? You came yourself and not armed?" carefully she put the helmet down. "You were serious about your offer?" her head dipped sideways, causing her hair to clink. She had thought it was a joke. He nodded and clicked. He knew his version of Cold Grid was not great, but he at least knew how not to insult them. He clicked affirmative again.

"I was. I am. You understand computers in a way that the rest of us can only dream of. And I think you would make a good addition to my crew." He turned his body toward her, an open gesture.

She click-trilled 'no' "If it's all the same, I know that kind of addition to the crew." She made a lewd gesture with her fleshy hand. "And I'd rather not." The click-trill of his was sharp and as close as the grid-language could come to disgust, "My crew doesn't work that way. You are there as my chief of security. Nothing else." His gaze was firm, but as was custom for the grid, he didn't break eye contact.

It was her turn again. She clicked a double note of curiosity. "How can you look on me?" she translated.

"You are not the first cold grid I've met." He used the word they used for themselves, 'Cold grid' or 'cold source' not Wraith, what the others called them. "GEM was a friend of mine. I rescued her and helped her get back to the Cold Grid."

She nodded, clicking lightly. Wonder, surprise, a sort of whirring click of awe. GEM was legendary, a being she might never see. "I can't go to the grid." Sad click, somewhere beyond sorrow, but somewhere before despair. "Not anymore. They" She clicked, a long sequence of what passed for swear words on the Grid. "They--did something to me, the doctors of the ladder-and-dagger." Her dark lips curled in disgust. "The grid makes me ill."

"Maybe we will be able to find a way to get you back." He trilled hope and then clicked caution. "But there will be--difficulties."

"Such as?" Curiosity again. Speaking in two modes, as this was called, was rare. There were few human or otherwise who learned to speak grid. And to find someone relatively conversant was rare, though to her his accent was that of a replimat or other service machine.

"Our mandate is to rescue, and some of those will include those your kind consider unredeemable."

"Units." The word was said with utter disgust. "I will trust your judgement on such things. But where are we headed?"

"Out there. "The click was actually a long string of clicks that meant 'everywhere and nowhere' the grid equivalent to 'far, far away.'

"We don't know how far, or how long. We don't know where we will be, we are to meet peaceably with as many as we can, but some will be worthy of your ire... And, within reason I'll let you

upgrade the systems so long as they are not a danger to the crew.
"

"Upgrade?" Curious trill, She smiled, her teeth an odd almost hematite. "You mean let me add Wraith Tech?" She said after a moment of frustrated clicks and ticks when she couldn't find the word she wanted.

"If we can get our systems to work together in a way that would not be detrimental to the crew." 'Not upgrade the warm-ware' the click said.

She nodded, before she had thought he was like every other captain, she had done her research, but to her most hot-source captains were the same, but this one, had come here, in her own place, and spoken to her like an equal, he had even attempted to use words she could easily understand. Not because he thought she was dumb, but to avoid any errors. He clarified anything that might later be a gray area.

"Go see the engineer about anything you need for health or computer safety, I know sometimes our computers and your system don't--play nice. "He smiled handing her the Padd and her security pass.

"Security will let you by as soon as it holds Atmo, if they give you any trouble let me know." She nodded.

"And make sure he puts a heat sink in your room. You need a place to recharge. Head of engineering may be able to make you some personal Atmo controls too. The Engineer is very good, and if anyone has a problem with you on my crew, you can tell them politely to step out the airlock and file a complaint. You are my crew, and you are a citizen."

"But besides, that, why me?" Curiosity. A click of worry.

He smiled.

She thought it looked sincere. His open stance never changed to a defensive shoulder-first stance, putting his body in line with his shoulder and facing her side-ways. He faced her chest-to-chest.

"Because you show them that we aren't like the ladder and dagger, no one could mistake you for Terran. And to show those who want to kill us that we mean business.

"Besides, you said you wanted to meet the Tucura; we're supposed to have six of their pilots training our Sudec pilots and engineers how to use the System." She was surprised to find he had read her file, but not just the official file, the logs she had put in too where she mentioned wanting to meet others. Being cold-source, as wraith identified themselves, she wanted to learn more, but she had to get over the—programs, pre-conceptions, as it were, that she came with.

"Thank you, captain, I am proud to face you, I will certainly log-on." Her words were a little off, but he understood her intent. Some ideas didn't translate the same in Wraith as they did in standard.

Best Pilot

"Captain Tyrell" as they called him had been arguing with the young man since they had hit the launch. It had taken fifteen minutes to drop to the ship, and now, as they waited for the airlocks to cycle manually, they continued their argument.

The young man, Ensign Thompson, was part of the crew assigned to make sure that whatever Captain Tyrell wanted, he got. Ensign Thompson's idea of "whatever he wanted" was slightly different though. The cut of his uniform made Tyrell uneasy, it looked very OSU, not at all the uniform he was wearing. And the shoulder patch, one he'd seen more and more often of late made no sense to him. "N4M31355." He assumed it was a platoon or a special project number, but it, and the attitude that seemed to follow anyone who wore it, set his teeth on edge.

"Look, the Admiral said anyone I want, and I want him."

"I don't think that he had a--" The young man stopped himself before the epithet made its way out. He'd been going to call him a "grifter", a somewhat derogatory name for a Girati. But the fact that this captain was also Girati sank in at the last moment and kept him from uttering the unforgivable.

"--A convicted criminal who deserted his last duty post in mind."

"Look, Ensign, to the OSU you are as much of a criminal as he is, and so am I." It was a shot in the dark, but by the way the young man stiffened, he'd hit very close to the mark.

"I know AJ's a bit rough around the edges, so am I. Hell, we took our Aja together on my steel. He's family, he's Kin, and he's the best damn pilot in the 'verse."

"And I think you are too close to him to judge. All I'm saying sir, is that you can't trust him to stay his post."

"Do you know why he abandoned his post?"

"No sir and it--"

"It does too matter," he shouted, stopping dead in his tracks. The timber of his voice made other people afraid of him. But for some reason this little Ensign, this Grazati pup, as his kind called someone who didn't know their place, didn't fear him or respect him, a bad place to be. "He abandoned his post because his orders were to murder civilians.

"He was ordered to take part in the Alpha Six massacre. Instead, he warned as many as he could and got down there in an escape pod to help as many out as he could before the gas hit. He's credited with saving ninety-three people. Many of them women and children."

"But he disobeyed orders."

"They were not lawful orders. You mean to tell me if you were ordered to space a civilian you would do it without question?"

"That is our job, isn't it?"

"Ona, no. Our job is to think for ourselves, and if the situation warrants it, to tell the powers that be what to go do with themselves."

"I won't argue with you sir, but you know my views." He let the captain go first through the doors and they waited while the lift cycled at reduced pressure too.

"Regardless, AJ is waiting on the bridge."

It took nearly an hour to get to the bridge, normally a ten-minute walk. The gravity controls were still being worked on and they had to stop and get Atmo gear. So the fact that the captain walked in with the silver bands around his neck and wrists didn't surprise anyone, except perhaps AJ.

AJ, on the other hand was standing in the middle of the bridge flanked by two Ground Patrol guards in full gear and rigged in magnetic restraints. Mag restraints were said to be the surest form of restraint. AJ looked like hell.

The guards were covered from head to foot, faceplate helmet in place, gloves, tied into their sleeves, shirts pulled down to their belts, boots tucked, and in one case, tied, spacer style; they were imposing. They were also in black, the color that OSU said made them invisible, made them nonentities, and marked them as Units. They were augmented humans with a military program capable of hijacking their bodies when their orders kicked in. They were kept in line with painful neural impulses called Reprimands.

Aconite Hyssop Jones, or "AJ" to his friends, had four things going against him. The first was that he was half Girati, the second was that he was half Resan, giving him odd looks and a frail form, third, was that he had spent more time in less than one third gravity and with a Resan metabolism, his muscles and bones would not acclimate well to space, but fourth, and most importantly, he had a big mouth and a short temper. It was this last pair of things that had put him where he was now, on the bridge of a ship in full mag-restraints, flanked by two zombies waiting to hear his fate.

Most Units didn't get the Zombie designation from him, that was reserved for the ones who no longer questioned, those who had given in to their fate, the broken ones so bent there was no hope of freedom even if the reprimands stopped forever.

At the time, the patches they wore on their arms meant nothing to the captain or the crew. A single black patch with white script N4M31355. They had all seen it; it was nearly ubiquitous in this sector, but no one knew what it was, and no one dared ask in case it was a holdover from the OSU. Their projects tended to have a way of causing death and destruction, or worse.

It was said that many of the Units were only Units because they had gotten a hold of classified material, Deep Black, as it was called. So deep, even the Highest Authority had no clearance. The OSU had a chancellor; the USL was in the process of putting together a democracy.

The only thing keeping AJ civil besides the fact that the gravity system that had been designed for him was not working, and he was malnourished, was the fact that the two blank-faced Units carried stun probes, and those things hurt. And in his current condition, a single touch from one of those could bring on a heart attack. His beautiful straw gold hair was lanky and in his golden, sunken almond-shaped eyes. His pointed ears looked too big for him, his head was down, arms crossed against his chest as the restraints required, and he fought to breathe in and out in a steady rhythm that would keep him conscious.

"What would be your pleasure, Captain?" The sarcasm dripped off of every word of inner-rim standard he spoke. Tyrell was taken aback, he'd never before had his friend act this way.

Either the boy was much worse off than he thought, or simply didn't know to whom he spoke.

Golden eyes squinted and rounded as he tried to force the figures into some sort of sense. The lack of air had made him nearly blind, for now, and the lack of sleep had done the rest.

"My pleasure will be that these two brain-dead Kam-ta leave you alone," he said smiling at his oldest friend.

His head lifted and the golden eyes squinted at him. The Girati was Rim Dialect, and older than he liked to admit, spoken with the ease of someone who used it all his life. The figure that had spoken was blurred and wore a uniform he didn't recognize, but the voice and the insult were unmistakable.

"Tyrell?" The voice was barely a whisper. And the captain wondered how many times this day had come in nightmare to pull a voice like that out of him.

"It's me old friend." His voice was soft, no rebuke or trouble, not yet. He could tell by the signs his friend was hanging on to his consciousness and sanity by sheer willpower. "You may unshackle him and go."

"With respect we have orders."

"Do you see that seal?" He pointed to the vid-screen still showing the USL seal because the system was offline. "That seal says you have no authority, so you have ten seconds to collect your shackles and get off my ship or I will put you in the brig."

They both blinked as the visors uplinked the conversation to the waiting ship, and they stiffened unnaturally awaiting orders. They received a recall command. A moment later, their systems reset, and they both jerked slightly. They blinked and knew what they had to do. They had to leave, with or without their prisoner. One of them undid the shackles while the other pulled off the vest. "He's all yours, but if we see him in patrol territory again in the next five years he will do hard labor at Aldis."

"Get off my steel."

The two Units packed up the things and hit a stud. There was an audible signal, a recall marker.

"Hold for transita" a disembodied voice said from the visor. It was projected so others could hear it too, so they wouldn't step too close and get whisked away. A moment later, after another, lower tone, the two men were gone in a flash of purplish light and a waft of cold air that smelled vaguely of despair.

Tyrell turned back to his friend as the two men vanished in the purple light. It didn't cross his mind at that second that it was an odd way to transport. Right at that moment, the only thing on his mind was his oldest friend, who quite frankly looked dead on his feet. "You look like last-week's trash."

"I feel like last year's trash," the voice that responded was broken, tired, not full of its normal fire. And he looked like he hadn't eaten in a week or more. He was fighting to stay upright, but was too proud to ask for help. The captain knew this but refused to embarrass him.

After a moment, he spoke to the captain. "With respect, what the hell am I doing here?"

"You're here to pilot this high-tech piece of space-garbage," Tyrell said with a smile. "But I don't want to see you on the bridge again for at least two days. An' that thing I owe you because of my daughter, we'll take a rain-day on that."

AJ nodded. "Yes sir." His salute was sloppy and over all, AJ moved like he was made of stone. The captain waited until he saw his friend turn to leave, then walked over to the comms unit since the voice controls were non-responsive yet.

"Tyrell to Medical,"

"Med-bay here." Came the oddly accented voice of the half-Tucuran.

"AJ is on his way down, please see he doesn't fall off the Maglift on his way down."

"Yes, sir."

That would keep the young man honest, make sure he actually went instead of going straight to his quarters. AJ paused long enough to make a lewd gesture in the Captain's direction, proof that, despite his situation, he was doing ok.

"I don't think Alis would agree." Tyrell said. "Go, before I have you removed." The threat was half-hearted, but it worked.

The Man Called Magic

The captain knew who the chief engineer was, or at least knew him by reputation, but nothing proved to him that the ship was still in bad shape more than when he saw the Chief engineer Som'a'son standing in the silver Atmo bands.

The Denvalian was huge. He towered over the captain by nearly head-and-shoulders and was almost half again as wide. Sometimes referred to as 'purple ogres' (never to their faces) they were seen as slow and clumsy and not very smart. But Som'a'son was as smart as they came and battle-hardened to boot. With benefit of a lower oxygen threshold, they were able to go where even the 'thin skinned' humans didn't dare. So finding him wearing Atmo bands was unsettling.

Atmo bands or "Atmosphere" bands were used to manipulate a gravity bubble, at least that was what they called it. It was far more complicated than that, but the bottom line was Atmo bands were like an EVA suit. They allowed you to breathe for short periods of time when there was no atmosphere. The longest the bands had ever lasted in space was 29 minutes. And it was the Avengers who set that record.

They were only worn on the ship when the atmosphere wasn't working. Hydroponics had just been put in, so they weren't producing air yet, and the canned system, "Breath" was not working efficiently because there were still hull breaches. So it was orders from engineering. Everyone wears Atmo. If the air handlers went out, they would have time to fix it before you died. That was a frightening thought, that the only thing between him and the nothing was a thin sheet of Duristeel and even that wasn't solid.

Chief Engineer Som'a'son, whom many of the humans called 'Sampson,' was a living legend. He was the man who had single-handedly flown a disabled freighter holding 72 cryogenically preserved crewmen through the Hulman minefield and to the Alpha colony worlds.

The freighter was not supposed to be able to fly through that minefield, and it wasn't supposed to have enough power to make it back to alpha. Not to mention he had rigged the asteroid lasers into CQWS.

His nickname was "magic," because they said that he could do just about anything. He was the man you wanted on a deep space voyage. The captain knew him, but they had never seen each other, just voice comms for nine hours one time while the captain was trying to save his ship, and So'ma'son had the part he needed.

He found Devalians to be shrewd diplomats and fierce competitors. They were also much stronger than even their hulking frames belied, and yet could move nearly effortlessly in null gravity. Most Denvalians were engineers and repairmen, going into the places that most other races needed hab suits to live.

While Atmo bands were not Denvalian in origin, they were heavily re-engineered by the crafty people to work better than they originally did.

So, seeing the man about whom it was said there was no feat of engineering that wasn't possible wearing gravity braces and atmo bands told him just how close to space they really were. And anyone who was born out near the rift knew that was never very far, and that one bad move, one misjudgment, could kill your entire crew.

"Ain' go' time for Landlubbers." He said in his pidgin spacer. The translator just beeped unable to keep up. "And this piece of klitspa is useless." He gestured at the pip on his collar that accessed the translator.

Denvalian Standard was hard to deal with on the best of days, so they chose to use Rim Standard, which was sort of a universal mother-tongue in the backwaters of the Universe like Denvalis. Denvalians had learned flight easily, though they often found little use for it themselves. They traded with many others who did, and so there were, as a result, Denvalian traders all over the Universe.

The word Landlubber always rubbed him the wrong way, though he knew in this case it was used without malice or knowledge. Captain Tyrell kept his answer civil and spoke pure Deep Rim standard.

"I ain' no landlubber. I've had steel since my Aja at twelve, an' I been out here longer than Girati coffee." The captain approached. "What's more, "I know my hand-over-hands, grew up on the Alpha run. Learned to bounce 'fore I could run."

The man turned and squinted at the reply in deep Rim Standard. He silently looked over the captain for a moment as he went over what the man said. To know your gravity drills as the USL called 'hand-over-hands' or the ability to move in less than Earth Gravity, and 'bounce' before you can run said a pilot has been out there a very long time. And the joke on Girati coffee added a century more. So, the man was a fair age, even for Girati, and still looked to be in his thirties. The man's face belied the brawling he'd done, and he was shorter stature like most space-born, shorter still because he sort of slouched ready for the gravity unit to fail at any time. That, and the set of his shoulders told him this had to be the Captain.

The giant smiled. "Som'a'son." He said, clasping the captain's arm. It was a Girati version of a hand-shake clasping forearms. "This must be your steel." He gestured expressively. "Anshas'a'an."

"Kimmsu." The captain replied absolving him of any offense. The man had no way of knowing he addressed the captain; they were still getting used to the new uniforms and ranks.

"Tyrell." The captain nodded. "Just came to see how she is. Sorry if my rim's a little rusty, haven't been out there in a couple light-years." His accent was thick, but perhaps a bit stilted.

"So my ears tell me." He switched to a slightly less pidgin form of the language. "And the translators haven't caught up yet with my rim language."

"Yeah, soon as we are safe we'll send linguistics down here." The captain said. There was nothing worse than not being understood. And this man, probably older than himself, had a heavy accent that was hard to defeat in newer standard.

The two men had spoken on comms but never seen each other, so it took a bit for Sampson to recognize the captain as the spacer he had met some time ago. His wife had mentioned Tyrell, but only in reference to his wife, her friend. Back when Tyrell had been freeing slaves in the rim, he'd come across Sampson's ship which was in a bad way after a raid, and the two had talked over comms while the crews had traded supplies, neither ship could come to the other because of the situation, Tyrell's ship had been under quarantine after a bout of the fever, and Sampson's could not hold a seal long enough to sterilize.

"The song tells me that AJ is here." It was more a statement than a question. The only thing that moved faster than freight on a Girati ship was scuttlebutt. Girati loved to gossip. And Devalians were nearly as fascinated with gossip as the Girati.

"You know AJ?" It shouldn't have surprised him, but it did.

"Who do you think made his Comps?" The man smiled, referring to the gravity compensators he was rarely without. "I met him out-" he gestured toward space. "Ain' sure where anymore to be honest. Somewhere far away from Denvalis and her children." He sighed. "But we did some trade, he got me parts I needed and I gave him his comps and passage out of the system."

"Passage out of the system" said it was probably slaver controlled. Or at least controlled by someone who didn't like him much. Sneaking out was always hard on AJ, he'd rather fight than sneak, but outgunned, out-manned, yeah... most freighters had no weapons except a laser for breaking asteroids and a few hand pulse pistols to protect themselves, a far cry from what most of the bandits had.

"By the by, atmo's still techy an' so is Gravity, but I rigged the lights to pulse 'fore the gravity goes normal again so they got time to orient. Cause even the best space-brat in the world can take a bad bounce."

The captain nodded, a precaution like that was prudent. "As soon as we are stable I also wanna do gravity drills, not normal for a ship this size, might give us an edge if we all know how to move and work in null, and some of these kids are a bit rusty. But most, if not all, have been rated deep space."

"That's good. But we got younglings about." Som'a'son smiled. His dark eyes and blue-tinged skin weren't off-putting in the least to the captain, but the captain was forced to either stand back or crane his head to look him in the face. His hair was jet black, and his skin, when he had been younger and in space his whole life had been more blue, but now it was tanned a deep purple with streaks of blue where the clothing was. He had married a retired Mistress. And though he knew the song, he didn't consider himself Girati, he'd never been blooded and never taken an Aja. Mainly because he was afraid the steel would reject him.

"Speaking of, how are yours?" The captain scratched his head. "How many is it now. Six?"

"Seven," he said with a smile. "My youngest, Caji just weaned, that was a relief, we didn't know if she would wean before her second incisors dropped. And Lumi just got posted to Anthricka."

The captain's face crumpled a bit, trying to remember the colonial geography. "That's the Winterland?"

The engineer nodded. "This ship should be space worthy in about three days, wouldn't try to space before four though; we still have a few hissers I can' find," he said, referring to bad seams or pin-prick leaks that made a hissing sound.

The captain nodded. "Is your wife with you?"

"Not yet, if we get near the Great Gathering, she said she would find steel to meet us. But she had to wait for the youngest to be weaned, feeding a youngling on steel is hard when they are Denvalian."

The captain nodded. "Then I wish her good journey."

"I will pass it along."

The hulking engineer walked down the gangplank pointing to the Atmospheric system, called Atmo, which he was only working on because the problems now were mechanical. "Breathers are working at 80 percent, but I plan to get that to optimum, and rebreathe system is at 71 percent. Pretty obvious it was sabotage." He frowned.

"Someone knew what they were doing to shut down the breather system, they destroyed the air return system and the scrubber sub-set. We had to replace it all, now its just trying to align it all again. Again, will have that functional by the time we space. Re-gen is online but its going to be a month or two before we can disengage Rebreath."

The ship had three oxygen systems, "Breath," the air handlers that used compressed and bottled air, "rebreath" which recycled the breathed air on the ship, and then the hydroponic air system which pumped co2 into the hydroponics bay and air out, into the regular breathing system, and then both "Breath" and "Rebreath" could be turned off. They would only kick in again if the air got too rare or if the hull breached.

He rounded the bulkhead to the secure doors and rapped hard twice before opening them. As a large frame, he needed room to walk, so he always knocked before coming through a bulkhead so they knew to get out of his way. The worst thing to hear on the ship was "Sampson's running, grab steel!" On his way to an emergency, he was known to bowl over smaller crewmen often without noticing.

"Dual core engine, it ain't tuned right yet, still a lot of vibration, but once she sings right, we should be able to out-fly anything out there. We have the input ports for the N-space needles." He leaned against a panel. "But it's going to take us another two days to finish calibrating the core. If she don't sing right before we space there will be a new sun in the galaxy. There's enough fissionable material that if it goes critical it could burn for a few thousand years, which is why we have a singularity on it. It goes critical we can dump it in the n-space thread, or a temporary singularity and it theoretically shouldn't hurt anyone."

"Then I will leave you to it." The captain said with a smile.

"You ever miss it?"

"Miss what?"

"The stone and the song?"

The captain's smile faded. "All the time, but I can't go back to that steel, not right now."

"I'm sorry," He put his large hand on his friend's back. "May her melody bring you only peace."

"Thank you, your condolences are appreciated."

The giant paused. "My wife won't make it harder will she?"

He nodded and then shook his head. "It will be nice having another singer on the crew. There are a few, but not many."

"Gen'shasha,." He said as he wandered off. The greeting or farewell translated roughly to "May all your dreams be of happy times."

Medicine

Doctor Stevens was nearly a legend in the outer colonies. Between his longevity, his immunity, and his looks when he was in his true form, everyone knew him. He was, after all the only half-Tucuran interspecies doctor with a degree in biological weapons and defenses.

He had just finished moving the last of his boxes into his quarters, as his mind did something he rarely allowed it to do. It thought back on a previous day. Specifically, the day that Captain Tyrell had called him up.

He still remembered that morning. He'd had tea and Raamik weed biscuits with it, a light mid-morning snack, waiting for his next patient. Instead, the short, stocky, slump-shouldered 'thin skin' had slumped through the door. He had stood there in his human-face, as his people called it. But the golden stone around his wrist gave away his heritage, even if nothing else did.

"What the hell are you doing?" Tyrell didn't seem angry, just annoyed. "I hire an ugly fish-face, I want an ugly fish-face." He straightened instantly, changing his view of the short man who stood in front of him. Even though he was nearly six inches taller than the captain, the Girati presence made him formidable and his eyes seemed to flash.

"Excuse me?"

"What the hell are you doing?" He asked again, more slowly this time. "I thought I hired an ugly fish-face for my doctor, not a human."

Stevens smiled, someone who knew how to talk to his kind was rare. He let the psychic picture fade. His skin turning an interesting if rather revolting shade between human and the mottled green-brown of the Tucura. Tyrell had just nodded.

"Not that I would think you would ever falsify your records the way you falsify your honors, but I need to talk about some of the duty stations you were on."

"What would a soft-skin know of honors?" He hoped the captain took the affront in manner in which it was meant, but he never knew, thin skins could take an insult to heart too often.

Tyrell laughed and shook hands. "I'm Captain Tyrell Hanson, but they call me Tyrell."

The doctor nodded, trading insults was restricted to greeting, the mistake that most soft-skins made. "Stevens Hrrg-lessep," he said with a smile. "But I go by Stevens." The amphiboid said. His face was Tucuran flat but he did have just the hint of the ridge under his nose so he could at least partially smile.

"You have deep-space experience, and I do mean in the more recent times than your Tucuran days, or the Academy."

Stevens nodded. "I have deep-space experience. I also scored tolerably on the hand-over-hand." He frowned. "But most of them liked my Human-face better."

"Good, well, unlike most of your duty postings, here, unless it is necessary because of bedside manner, or obligation, you may stay in your true form as often as you choose."

The captain smiled again and looked over at the officer in front of him. "I know it's kind of a touchy subject, but as we

Humans define the term, do you define as male, female, intersex, or other."

He hated questions like this, but it was better to get the pronouns right now. Tucurans had two sexes and five genders, so it was easy to see where the captain was coming from.

"From your point of view I would define as male. And I prefer male pronouns." The Tucurn half-smiled. "So, you are familiar with Tucuran Culture?"

"Enough to know mucking up the pronouns is a no-no and that it's easier to ask than to offend a Tucuran because they have *very* long memories and lots of very powerful weapons." The captain put down the file. "I must say I was surprised to see your name as a doctor, I would have expected you as a pilot."

"Why?"

"Because I know the best ships are Tucuran. And because I know medicine is not always a Tucuran past time."

It was the doctor's turn to smile, that was perhaps the most tactful way he had ever heard it put. Tucurans were known as the most battle-hardened space fleet in the known universe. The only ones worse were the Casandi, but they rarely left their world.

"That was well-played. It's obvious you have traded insults with my kind before."

"I'm Girati, we trade lots of things with lots of people." His face fell for a moment as the reason for him not being on his Girati ship raced back to the front of his mind, and he forced it away again, changing topics before the Doctor could ask his steel or house name.

"You showed an amazing aptitude for interspecies medicine and for biological defense," Tyrell said. "We are heading out into deep space on a mixed cruise."

"Do you mean that as men-and-women or as multi-species?" He thought he would clarify just in the interest of full disclosure.

"Both, we are a mixed crew without Moiety." He clarified, forgetting that Tucuran has both. He shifted, "If you don't mind me asking," he gestured pardon. "How did you manage to avoid the xenophobia that is so common among your kind?"

The doctor smiled. "Not hard when you spend most of your young life being made fun of because you looked like a soft-skin, but when the stone chose me, despite their objections, some of my people were a little less—annoying." He pulled the cuff off and twisted the silver bands back into the circlet he usually wore and settled the amber stone between his wide-set and nearly pupilless eyes.

"It is hard to argue with a stone-bearer and win. And then the fact that as a half-human I have better control over our gills than they do."

The captain snorted. "They still think they are Vestigial?" He only noted that because it could come in handy if they ended up in any watery worlds.

The doctor nodded. "How long is our mission?"

"Indefinite." Tyrell smiled. "We are looking for some of the lost colonies."

"Why?" The half-Tucuran's face twisted into curiosity and not-quite disgust.

"Because it's been far too long, we want to see how they are doing, and what they have made for themselves. We want to extend the olive branch in hopes of being able to trade with them, and maybe learn a bit more about ourselves."

"So, the mixed crew is also to prove that we aren't like the Ladder-and-dagger."

"That's a good way of putting it." He hadn't heard the patrols called that in a while, the Purity Patrols emblem was the helix of DNA split by a dagger.

"And if we meet up with them, they are to be apprehended by whatever force is necessary. However, because you are a medical officer we will still expect you to follow USL medical guidelines."

Stevens snorted. The Tucura were also notorious for 'testing' theories on patients. "Understood sir." It was clear the captain had read his file, his complete file.

"Incidents like Beklis 4 will never happen again, is that clear?"

"Crystal, sir," The half-smile faded under the wilt of the Girati glare from the captain. There were few creatures, human or otherwise, who could frighten him, but this man did, because he could see the steel in his eyes. He'd be willing to space him if it meant saving his crew. "We have an understanding."

"Doctor?" The captain stood in front of him, looking worried. "You didn't hear a thing I said, did you?"

The doctor frowned, another human habit. "No, I must admit I was lost in my memories, a habit from my mother's side, I'm afraid." He smiled that almost-smile of his. "I assume you are here about your friend?"

"Yes, why does he look so bad?" He walked over beside his prone friend. His skin was the wrong tone, his hair lanky and thin, and overall he looked like he hadn't eaten in years.

"He's been held in two gee without his compensators and on a restricted diet." He sighed. "The little bit of food they have been giving him were all strong meats and alcohol, two things he's not supposed to have large amounts of." The captain frowned. Red meat and alcohol would make him violently ill. He was missing an essential protien for breaking down red meat. It was actually a disorder found in lots of species, but his Resan side made the tablets that he would have to take to compensate dangerous to take too often.

"Is he out?"

"I sedated him. He's also on a systemic rejuvenator set to Resan-Spacer normal. The system should shut down in…" He leaned over to check the controls. "Ten hours, I'm going to keep him sedated for at least the next three days, since launch isn't for five." He also has been on a Thulian day."

"Forty-two-hour day?"

His eyebrows crawled up and pulled together as surprise and anger warred on his features. They had been torturing him. It was a form of torture that was hard to prove because they could claim that they didn't know about his condition, though AJ never hid it.

"Is that causing trouble?" The doctor nodded. "His system can't synch. He's having temporal synchronicity issues. Not recursion like a traveler, but his system doesn't know if it is night or day."

The doctor paused a moment before he asked gently. "Does AJ follow the discipline of Altiiu?"

"Last time I checked he did, but admittedly I lost touch with him last time I went out-system. I honestly thought he was still on the Vega run."

The doctor nodded. He would have to keep to discipline until AJ could tell him otherwise. Altiiu was similar to some of the old-terra restrictions against certain diets and certain activities.

"Something else you should know." He pulled the captain over to one of the other screens where a faded, blown-out image could be seen. The green ink had faded but he could just make out the Vega V crest.

"It looks like his ship was captured by slavers. That looks like a worn Manumission mark on the back of his shoulder. There are signs that he had to have the mark removed and redone, because they were done with Ferrous inks, and Resan's are seriously allergic to high amounts of ferric compounds. The original manumission mark would have been brown-red. Made by inking with ferrous oxides. And one or both of you spent time in the rift between now and then, because your ten years is closer to twenty."

The fact that he'd been in and out of slavery bore out the fact that by his count it had been a decade or more since the two had seen each other. He didn't relish the news he had to tell his friend. Any of it. And now, to find out that what had been ten years for him had been closer to twenty for his friend... That hurt.

"Are people aware of his condition with food?"

"He will tolerate red meat twice a year, on his birthday and on the day his mother died. There are Girati dishes he likes but won't otherwise eat."

The doctor nodded. "He seemed pretty wary of you."

"He married my daughter and broke her heart; I promised him when I saw him again I owed him a good right cross."

"Divorce?"

"No, he couldn't stay on the ship. He hasn't seen his wife in twenty turns or more, and not because he hates her, the stone doesn't like him, and she's the mistress, for ship harmony, she had to throw him out. But he also has a son he has never seen."

The captain swallowed. A son by now who would be grown. Ten years had suddenly become twenty, and depending on where his son was, maybe more.

"So, he doesn't know." His eyes belied a sorrow too deep to tell. He'd wait until his friend was better. He hadn't heard it in ten years, a few days or weeks more wouldn't hurt anyone. In fact, if he never had to tell him, never had to watch that look again, he'd do almost anything.

The doctor touched the screens again, "He's also got degenerative Choira."

Tyrell choked on his own air. Choira, if left untreated was deadly. He had known about it for a long time, but every time a doctor said those words, it was like a blow to the solar plexus.

The doctor held up his hand. "Fortunately, it's still in the early stages and can be corrected without a graft." The doctor smiled his flat smile, but it looked worried.

"However, that presents us with a slight problem." He turned to the captain to get his attention. "Do you know his blood-culture? I can't type him, and he will need regular transfusions for the next... maybe six months. The procedure should slow, or possibly stop the disease, especially if we can find a Donor with a graft or who survived."

"You won't be able to type him. Being half-Resan he has more than the standard cultures. The Girati have the standard human types and the Resa have the three Resan types so he ended up AOGeb."

"So, an oddball all the way around. A'geb is hard to find. I'll have to make sure I have some on standby. He has one of three types we can't synth."

"Agis'a might have some supply. And we will be heading that way too. So maybe you can have some sent and pick up more on the way out."

The doctor nodded. "I take it you've had this conversation before?"

"Many times since we found out he had it. His mother died from the Fever brought on by Choira. We couldn't give her the culture to save her because it would make the fever worse."

"I'm sorry."

"So am I." He smiled wanly, remembering the trouble the two of them got into. He turned to walk away before turning back to the doctor.

"When he's stable, send him to me."

"Yes, sir."

Old Friends

AJ WAS BACK IN his quarters by now. Sleeping peacefully, but the captain stood outside his door for nearly ten minutes before turning away and finding other pursuits. He'd had the conversation in his mind a million times, and some went better than others. But how did you tell the man who was your best friend, who'd stood second at your wedding, and who had been pleased to marry your daughter, that everything he had known was gone? That everyone who ever knew him except the captain himself was no more?

And how did he tell him that his wife, his beloved Alis, was gone, lost in a raid ten years ago? That the Captain's choices had damned her and everyone else on that ship? It didn't surprise him that he found himself in the common room and seated at the bar. He held up his hand and just said, "Tem'il'a" the barkeep nodded and poured two drinks, one staying on the counter the other going to the captain. It was a Girati custom. They would pour a drink for whoever was in their thoughts, and if someone sat down to drink it, they would tell them why they were there. With that many telepaths and empaths on a ship, keeping your guard up was a must, and Tem'il'a "a drink of two" told them that someone needed to talk.

The other person couldn't judge, just listen. No one sat with him, and at the end of the night, he drank the second shot, turned the glass upside-down, and said the prayer of closing. The only person he wanted to talk to was AJ, but the only person he didn't want to talk to was AJ.

Telling him would open the wound for himself too, and he was afraid that the grief might overwhelm him again, and he couldn't do that, not again. He couldn't afford that, not without endangering his own steel.

The rest of the night he spent in the cargo bay, he brought a ball and wore himself out with null-gravity handball, until, he hoped the dreams would leave him be.

AJ sat on his bed, he'd been trying to read, but he couldn't. His brain and heart knew what he didn't want to understand. Tyrell didn't want to tell him his wife was dead. But he didn't have to, at least, he didn't have to to let him know for the first time. AJ knew. He'd known since the day it happened. He wanted to talk to him, to share the misery, but he himself barely knew how to deal with the pain, he couldn't imagine that blinding pain on his friend, especially since he lost not only his daughter, but his wife of a hundred years.

Her song, always strong and clear, had become worried, and then vanished all together. There was only one reason for that. She was gone. Died, and as angry as he wanted to be, he couldn't be.

He was angry at Tyrell, and he wasn't. Slavers were nasty bastards, and the ship refused to be taken. They fought to the man, trying to repel the ship and its invaders before they were able to leave. He didn't know if they got any prisoners, but the damage was done, the ship was damaged, and the crew was left dead and dying.

AJ's world had stopped spinning, and he had done everything he could to get himself arrested or killed. And he didn't know if it was good, bad, or just odd that after ten years of running, he had run into the one man he wasn't sure he was ready to see.

They'd taken their Aja together, and he'd stood Second at Tyrell's wedding, they were as close as men could be, brothers, family, but right now, the sight of one brought back misery to the other.

Maybe they'd go put some gloves on and knock each other senseless, maybe they would just drink and cry. He didn't know, but as much as he wanted the captain to come so he could have the conversation, he didn't.

He knew only bits and pieces of what happened, gleaned from the song. His wife, as the mistress, was always in the song. But without enough crew, the ship was dead in space.

Finally, he reached into the nightstand and took the pills his doctor had given him. They were sleep aids, ones that allowed him to sleep without trapping him in the dream. His hand hesitated for a moment, with the tab halfway to his mouth. He'd been having a new dream. Not really a nightmare, but a strange dream. A dream about a girl. A girl that set his teeth on edge. But he needed sleep, and he didn't want to be drugged by the doc again. So, he pulled out the sleeping tab, put it under his tongue and drifted off to sleep, hoping for a decent dream for once.

Old Enemies

Gabriel Rican, the once-captain of the ship that bore his name, had pulled some strings, and he had a young man brought in.

"You got yourself assigned to the Rican?"

"Yes, sir, though outside this room I'm not allowed to call it that, and I can't stand the captain."

"This Tyrell guy?" Gabriel asked.

"Yes, sir. He and I had some words the first day." He frowned. "He called up AJ, who was supposed to be on his way to Aldis. But the captain pulled strings and got him sent to the ship. So their Pilot, fourth in command, is a treasonous coward who abandoned his post and disobeyed orders."

"He doesn't know you are here?" Gabriel asked.

"No, sir, and he doesn't know about the modification, neither does the... creature that runs security. She's the one I have to worry about. If it figures out what I've done it might space me itself." He would never deign to call a creature like that a 'she'.

"Once they get past the system, say two, three days out, I want you to trigger the system. I don't want the ship making it to Epsilon to get the Needles."

"I also got the DNA files you wanted." He handed over the chips. "I'm not going to ask, but I got most of them. Couldn't get the chief of security, medical or the Engineer, too hard to get close to and if this is for what I think it is, non-humans just gum up the works." Ensign Thompson smiled. "But if it helps, the pilot, AJ, he's got Choira, and certain drugs will make it worse. But be careful or you will get another visit from your—friends who took your ship. Rumor has it he worked with them for a while."

Gabriel had heard the rumor that AJ had once been an Avenger, and while he didn't believe the IRT would allow such stolen valor, he didn't know how that could possibly be true. "Why would they want a creature like that?"

"I don't know, but be careful, this guy, Reaper, he can make you disappear with a few words. And he has friends. Also, one of the division leaders in the small ships, Sudek or whatever they call them, I swear he's Old man Jeffries' boy. A slave runner."

Jeffries had heard all the rumors of the IRT known as the Avengers, and from what he knew Gabriel had been treated like a prince by them. That did set a little ill with him. Why were they so nice with him?

"That's good to know; maybe we can use that against him. You'd better get going before they notice you are gone." Gabriel said as he slipped the last part of the file he needed. "Don't come back here again."

"Yes, sir."

If he'd been a history buff, he might have said "keep your confederate money boys, the south will rise again," but he didn't.

That, however, was their belief that whatever had happened would be undone and they would get the galaxy back, and put it back on track.

"Major." The file was clutched in a near death-grip. The young man held out a scanner and waited. No words other than to call the man by his title. The young man was standing free arm at his side visor over his face.

"What is it?" Major Hunter was just testing to see what the young man knew of the project.

"Just said it needed to be delivered. No ears, no eyes."

Mike Hunter, aka Reaper, put his thumb to the scanner and it trilled, the young man turned the envelope over to show the seal.

"Please note the seal is intact." It was a rote response.

"Yes, it is." He took the file out of the Unit's hand and flipped it open, not even waiting to dismiss him.

"You thought about my job offer?" the major asked. He looked up at the visored young man who stood before him.

"You are serious about that? I mean, that it would get me out of—" He gestured helplessly to himself.

Major Hunter nodded. "Yes, it would. It would get you out of everything, and since we all wear black here, you would be free. You'd never have to go back." He held out a hand. "And I have he clearance to make it stick."

"Yes, but I don't think my ma—"

Mike walked over to the comm unit. "What's Your designation kid?" He cut him off before he could call the man who used him his master. A designation Major hunter detested."

"4561." The young man said, tilting his head sideways as he saw Major hunter type something on the computer.

"The file's on our findings of Alpha six by the way." Then he smiled and punched the button for Comms. The smile on his face told the Unit something was up but for a moment he was frightened that maybe this man was exactly his name. "Reaper."

Mike gestured to a seat. "would you like a drink?"

"Sir?"

"You have just been exposed to classified information. You cannot leave this room without proper clearance." Major Hunter took a drink of his coffee and pulled an EMP pistol which he palced on the desk between them. "So, you have two choices. Either way you are free."

"Scotch." The young man said. Major hunter got up and poured a drink.

"You wouldn't be able to stop me would you?" Mike asked as he put the drink in the young man's hand and sat on the edge of the wooden desk.

The young man took a sip of his scotch and looked around at the historical military posters on the wall. For a moment he ignored the question."

"Would you?" Mike asked quietly.

"No sir. Even my Primary Function program cannot trump direct order.

He picked up the gun and placed it against the young man's chest.

He didn't move, barely seeming to breathe Finally the boy said quietly. "Not there" He put the glass down and turned the chair until the gun was against the back of his neck. "Best shot is right there."

"Is this what you want?" Major hunter asked. He wasn't sure if there was enough fight left in the Unit to deal with what came after. "Because I don't think it is, but I need you to tell me. You can't just meekly comply."

There was no movement or sound for a long moment. Mike had just about decided there was nothing left of the actual human under the program. And then the boy spoke.

"I want to be free." The five words hit the young man like a thunderbolt. Major hunter darted up and hit a hidden button on his desk, watching as the boy slumped in relief.

"I'm sorry. I had to test you."

"Free." all the boy could do for a moment was sob the single word.

Major hunter nodded and put the glass back in his hand. "Take a drink. It will settle your nerves. The reprimand isn't over, but we've blocked it until we can get you to medical."

"Records," Major hunter snapped, in the clipped tone he used for the computer. "Please send word to 4561's former owner of record, that there is no longer any such entity."

"Your name is Sebastian." Mike said as he opened the door to admit the blonde doctor. "His name is Curtis, but we call him Cyborg."

"23?" The young doctor just smiled. "I don't use that designation, but I can help you break the program that is trying to kill you."

"How?"

"That file?" Mike pointed to the one he had open on the table. "I told you the name, and I know that mirror is placed so you can see the paper whether you know or not." Major hunter smiled. "We've been rescuing Units for a long time. We've already sent a crew for your wife and children. They will join you in a day or so when you are out of quarantine.

"Your status as a Unit is null. You have been classified Ultra Black which means if you want to call yourself Sebastian, they can't stop you. They also can't arrest you or take your rights."

Maiden Voyage

The whole ship felt different. It was alive. Even if its engine wasn't running, the ship itself was nearly electric. There was so much buzz and positive energy that the ship itself seemed to hum. And that change in tempo had woken the captain, long used to being attuned to any change in mental state on his ship. The excitement was nearly palpable.

It was still early when the captain woke, so he stood in his new quarters looking out. He'd been assured by Sampson that there were no more breeches and he felt confident enough to remove his Atmo bands. Though he still felt uneasy. He'd had the dream again. The girl. And there was something, if he was on his own steel—his Girati steel, maybe he would know what was wrong, but right now, he just had foreboding he couldn't shake.

Finally, he went to the bridge. The obligatory "Captain on the bridge" made him smile.

"As you were."

He took his seat, looking at the new USL emblem, the starburst and olive branches, the start, they hoped, of a galactic empire of peace and freedom.

"Where are we?" He'd had this conversation with his crew before, so by now, they knew he meant in Launch Protocol.

"We were just about to light up the internal sensor system. Once Bios is online, we will have full security control," Jenna said. Bios was "Biologic Information and Operations System." It was the internal sensors, the habitat control, and the navigation console. Bios was also supposed to end the chance of imposters by being able to match identi-chip signatures from previous postings.

It wasn't often, but sometimes people would switch chips to get on a better ship. Of course, it didn't always work for clones or twins, but it was better than manual system. BIOS would also keep all medical data current and be able to call ahead to systems that were linked to get them supplies.

"Turn it on," the captain said,

"BIOS is Online," Jenna's voice said from the console near the captain. Having the security officer behind him always made him feel safe. "Scan in progress, baseline acquired." Her modulated human voice spoke in a melodic whisper that filled the entire room.

Because of her implants, her uniform was more a tabard and pair of pants than an actual shirt. And then the bands on her wrists and ankles kept her from accidentally hurting the computers, and also kept the air around her at a comfortable forty-two degrees. As even a partial Wraith, she had no ability to control her temperature; she had spent her formative years on the cold grid. But when, after two or three years, she was still a baby, they sent her 'hot-side' to the real world. Most Wraith-kind had to grow up in the hot worlds or they would never age. While she was here, the OSU and particularly, Gen-Tech had experimented on her.

"All scans are normal, Captain, all crew accounted for, no stowaways." She had checked the reading twice, unable to shake the feeling that something was wrong, and the word Nameless.

Maybe it was just the omen of a ship without a name, though technically they had one—their new hull numbers.

"All right, stow and secure all weapons, rotate CQWS to launch position and make sure the rail-bays are locked and stowed."

The Close Quarters Weapon Systems, or "See Cows" as they were called, were small rail guns that could be retracted into the hull, during launch they had to be rotated 180 degrees and retracted or the force of the launch would rip them clean off.

Those and the small fighters were some of the new enhancements that the ship had. She still looked like a patrol ship, had the same vague shape, but everything was different.

She had the same hull plates, but new shields, new weapons, and a new type of core. And they hadn't even brought the main defense cannon online yet. They wanted to wait until they were out at the rim. Where there were enemies worth more than target practice before, he lit that up.

Weapons storage, bays 1, 2, 5, and 9 would lock automatically during a launch and so would the rails so there was no possible way to get to the weapons during launch, and the rail launchers were locked down to prevent anyone from being able to launch. But the thing that worried the captain the most wasn't the possibility of losing the guns or of accidental launch, but the ever-gnawing threat to his crew of sabotage. The reason he had called Jenna in was she was the one most likely to catch a saboteur because she knew the most about computers on a purely computer level. She was one. She could communicate with every computer on the ship at once, and she could synthesize that information as she worked. Often times, however, she would find the trouble and not understand what the trouble was. Which was why the word Nameless struck her as odd and random. It was so random it had to be specific. Jenna dragged her attention back to the display, realizing that the captain was waiting for her. "Storage 1, 2, 5 and 9 are locked, Sudec are put to sleep, and rails are locked and stowed." She spoke only slightly louder with her musical voice.

"Security reports we are stowed and ready to get underway, sir." Nav was online, AJ sitting there grinning like an idiot.

"Good."

Main screen on," the captain said. The display snapped to life for the first time. It was dim because they were still on station reserve power. "Send the inversion wave to start the main processors."

The inversion wave was the first step to starting the engine. The wave would wake the onboard computer system and flush out any program remnants left from upgrades. It also set up the polarization field that became part of the hull and the outer shield. The energy from the wave would be siphoned off into coils around the ship and used to reinforce the hull plates, and drop their relative mass, a trick learned from the

Girati. Everyone's hands raised from their stations, if connections were going to blow, they would blow now. A few stations sparked, but none went dark, and no fires started.

"Inversion wave sent."

"Systems responding. Bridge systems functioning."

The captain waited for a silent ten count. "Increase the wave the rest of the ship."

"Aye, captain." He punched in the codes. "Wake sent, BIOS online."

Again, hands went away from stations as they pulsed. There was a tone that went deck by deck just before the wave, signaling them to step away from the stations while they were started. Hands left the slick screens, and a few took a step back, in case of sparks.

"Switch Comms to Internal control."

"Internal, aye."

There was a loud squelch as the lines changed over. "Sorry, sir." The communications officer smiled tightly. It was a rookie mistake, forgetting to disconnect before switching.

"Opening the channel again."

"Galbraith station this is USL ship 2019, we request permission for main system start and station disengagement."

"Captain Tyrell, it's good to hear your voice. You have permission for main system start and station disengagement." It was all a formality. The engine was now primed, the computer was online, and the hull plates charged to drop their mass enough that they were now not tightly moored.

"You heard the man Som'a'son, let's light this candle."

The core was complicated. It was a gravity drive driven by the power of two spinning cores in tight orbit around each other. As long as the cores spun, there was more power than could be calculated. They were, in essence, miniature suns, A tiny binary system that produced a gravity well that powered them.

The whole timbre of the ship seemed to change. Instead of the constant thrum of the workers, there was a very pronounced vibration as the core came online. The comms chirped as Engineering started their report as soon as power was flooded their way.

"Main breakers have engaged. Power density within expected norms." They had made dry runs with the system unpowered, but it needed system power to kick-start it. As long as they could get the two cores rotating properly, they would have all the power they could ever need. The voice on the coms was slightly delayed by the translator.

"All right boys, throw the switch and engage the first core."

There was silence for a moment.

"Main power sequence starting. Core one has begun to spin." The voice was one of the ensigns. There was a long pause. "Systems are nominal. Power output at sixty percent and climbing." The ship rocked. Then it rocked again, harder.

"Just a synch issue. It will be fixed in just one tic." The voice was the slightly delayed voice of Som'a'son. "There we go. Timing is fixed."

There were no more jolts.

"Start the second core." Som'a'son said. The second core, like its own little sun, began to spin, and then slowly the two spinning balls began to rotate around each other. "Watch the distance."

"Primary, secondary, and tertiary rotation stable, the core is started," one of the engineers said.

"Primary orbital rotation of cores has started." The engineer sounded happy, as if he had just had an eighth child. "Rotation is stable, we have main engine turnover, Captain."

Bank by bank, lights and terminals began to switch over from station power to internal. And for just one moment, a few people thought they saw the ghost of an image, gone before they could even process what it was. N4M31355. The same number that had been showing up around the station.

"Breath and Rebreath are internal, gravity—internal." The bridge crew ticked down the list.

"Main engine is up to cruising speed; output is steady at one half-billion light-ohm."

"Navigation, do we have the buoy?"

"We have the signal loud and clear."

"Good, give me an internal channel please."

"Aye sir, internal channel open."

"Crew of the USL ship 2019, I wish we had a fancier name to go with this auspicious occasion, but we don't. What we do have is a daunting mission, to reconnect with the lost worlds driven away from us by the great Galactic war. And to bring peace to those worlds still fighting it.

We don't go out there to find a new and better world, though we may, We don't go out there to find out what kind of men and women we are, we don't even go to safeguard the future of our world, though that may wait out there, too. We go out there to face the things that we, as a race, have done, to ourselves and others, and to do what we can to fix it.

"We do not go for ourselves but for those we may save by our going."

That was imprinted on the hulls of the colony ships that left Earth during the war. And they left with the promise in their ears that we would follow them one day when the war was over, and we would let them know we had survived. So in the words of my ancestors, the First Flight, "Onward to the stars and all that waits beyond them." He pressed the button to close the channel.

"Retro thrusters at 1/4 when the station feed starts."

"Aye captain!"

The ship bucked a bit as the station feed started. The docking clamps were still engaged. And the station was moving, changing. The circular arms that had surrounded them were opening like a flower as the bay got longer and longer. Once the arms had locked and the rail was as long as it would go, the system powered the launch rail.

Like most ships of its size, 2019 could rail launch. They were capable of atmospheric launch, but this was much faster way when you couldn't use N-space.

"Station reconfiguration is complete, we are go for Launch."

"Retro thrusters to half, station keeping." The captain replied.

"We have launch signal." The pilot still looked like the underside of a reef speeder after hitting iron coral, but he was on his feet and his hands were steady. His golden eyes were mostly the right color, and his gravity compensators blinked their steady rhythm.

"AJ, Launch."

The ship jolted forward and was suddenly in open space.

"Station aft ten thousand meters and retreating." He said calmly. Launch was always the hardest for him, not because of fear but excitement.

"We are go for main-engine switch-over," he said quietly.

"Main engines online, cruising speed reached."

"Lock in a course for the belt, we still need to get our needles."

"Aye sir, at current speed that will take us nineteen days."

"Let's nudge that up. Triple-light, please."

"Aye-sir, triple light." He tapped the controls, stopping to rap on the side of the console, a good-luck habit most Girati had.

The comm from Engineering chirped before the captain could ask for a report and Som'a'son was almost unintelligible with excitement.

"She's singing captain." The engineer called to the bridge. "No sign of strain. She isn't even bothered by triple light."

"It better not be, she's rated for twenty-light, but we need a hell of a reason to use that. The only issue is going to be going irrational into N-space."

The only reason she was only rated twenty light is because they didn't know if the ship would hold together any faster in normal space. They were less concerned with the engine than the ship. As long as the cores spun there was unlimited energy, the problem was not shaking the ship to pieces.

Walker of the Sands

Normally, the first officer was the first one he would talk to, but the man he had asked to join them had been delayed. He was one of the last. The figure that stepped through the door brought a waft of the strong scent of Amara, and the tall, dark-skinned man was swathed head-to-foot in dark traveling robes and wore a breather face mask.

After a moment he unclipped the breather and stepped out of his traveling cloak, hanging it over his bag, he turned to face the captain. The ship had to swing by and pick him up at Lexaris, after he got called home to Amara. The captain knew such a call didn't come often, and when it did, you didn't dare ignore it. So, it was 19 hours after launch before they had a first officer.

The cloaks had a little bit of "magic" as most people said, standing up on their own when placed over the bag. It allowed them to take the coat off and not worry about it. In reality, it was a fabric that turned rigid when it cooled to air temp and when heated to body temperature was malleable.

"Captain, I beg your indulgence for the robes, but your message caught me on an important matter of my kind." His smile was sincere, but he was unsure if he should shake or salute being so out of uniform.

"Lieutenant Commander Toru," Captain Tyrell placed his hand over his heart and bowed, as was tradition among the Shedda. "I'm honored to finally meet you. If you wish to remain in your robes, you are allowed."

The traditional traveler's greeting surprised him. He would not have pegged this man as brusque and burly as he was to be a "friend of the path." The accent in his ears rang as deep rift—he'd have to check that later—but if that was true, he was a very long way from home. The deep rift was months' travel at sub-light, years if you got delayed by food and fuel issues. This ship could make the trip in a week, but who knows how long it would have been on the worlds of the Rift.

Toru shook his head. "The sand does not blow as heavily here," he said with a smile. "And I find them rather cumbersome in ship life, but the collar remains."

Tyrell nodded. "You are welcome on this steel. May your way be easy, and your circle be long before you go to the outer pathways."

Now he *knew* the man was a Friend of the Paths. And a good one to know both the greeting and the blessing. Someone who they trusted. He smiled. "I had no idea you knew how to speak to a Keeper of the Way."

"I've had many of them book passage on my steel. Night Flame is my Girati steel, but she was somewhat damaged a while ago and I have not repaired her yet."

His song sang of sadness and anger, and so Toru decided not to ask any more. But the ship name was known to them. "She is known to us as free steel." He smiled. "That marks you as free-singer then? That you leave ship and stone?"

"Yes, it does, and yes, I am a free-singer, cousin to the singers of the Sand."

That he knew that marked him as a Girati from the deepest part of space, what they called the keepers of history, but even the mention of stone and song brought a crashing sadness that made him wary of asking more. Whatever it was was something that had nearly destroyed this man.

For a moment he wanted to ask more, to ask about the dream of the Girati he had been having, but the overwhelming sadness tempered his curiosity. Better to ask another day. Maybe his own master knew more.

Toru picked up the bag, and they started down the way to his quarters, but it was clear to see that the ship was far from ready to make a long voyage. Though it was finished, there were many things that still needed to be broken in. They were not yet ready for travel outside the local distances for help.

"The ship is in some disarray." He frowned. "And so is it's crew. Many discordant songs."

"Yes," the captain replied. "She was very nearly scuttled. Her crew is good, though some are rough. All I ask is that you avoid fighting if you can, and by you, I mean the crew in general." He smiled at the near slip. "But some of the crew are wanted men, will that go against your sensibilities?"

Tyrell was always sensitive to the needs of others. And the last thing he wanted was to breed discontent, so he figured he would be as upfront as he could. The thought of AJ and his two open contracts came to mind.

Toru held up a hand to stop him. "Not as long as they are wanted for the right reasons. A just man fears no one, the unjust fears all. It is not my place to judge. I can only know them by their circles, and since you have known many of them, like the pilot who weighs so heavily on your mind, for so many years, I must defer to you to their path more than I."

The captain smiled. "Am I broadcasting that loudly?"

"You are Captain. But even were you not, it would be easy to understand you. You have his file clutched in your hand, and I assume you are looking for answers."

"My friend is in a bit of a bad way, and I wanted to know if it was all incarceration or if other things brought him to this place." He was worried. He'd browsed the file but not in depth before. He wanted to take it and read it, to fill in the blanks since the last time he'd seen him.

"You should speak with him."

"He is never good at talking. Too much of his father in him. And besides, the doctor told me in no uncertain terms that he'd space me if I upset him before next week. He's still very weak.

Toru nodded. "I cannot say that he will be ok, I have no right to promise that, but I can say that I wish him no ill will. I will remember him in my prayers tonight."

"Thank you, Toru."

"And Captain, I don't know what it means, but something has come to me every night since your call. "Beware the Nameless."

"I know it is not this ship but has something to do with this ship." He shook his head. "It is all curves and circles, and I cannot see the truth right now."

"Thank you for the warning."

"Curves and circles." The captain said under his breath. The way a Shedda spoke of a puzzle. Curves and circles but you could not yet see the outline.

"Walk softly, strike true, and may you eschew the walking of the darkest path until you return to the outer circles."

"And you Captain." Toru said, nearly lost in thought as they parted ways to their own quarters.

Nameless

A. Hughes walked into the captain's office and saluted. She stood six-three and was broad shouldered, square jawed, and not the obvious choice for a female. And seeing the captain, a Girati, she worried that she was in for more trouble because of her gender.

"Aaron, please tell me why the governor of New Zion is asking to have you extradited to New Zion and hanged for treason." There was no preamble, the captain didn't look up from his desk where he was busy looking through the file— the wrong file.

It figured that her last duty post would send *his* file to the captain. And now the Governor of the New Zion colony was trying to take her back.

"It's Abigail, sir," She took a deep breath. "And, technically I am guilty according to the charter of New Zion, which is why I left New Zion."

She smiled tersely. "Changing your sex or gender is an affront to God, the Church and life itself, not to mention the government of New Zion, so when I re-enlisted, I was arrested for treason."

"And your file?"

"Sir?" She wasn't sure what he was asking about her file.

"Why hasn't any of this been reflected in the file?"

"Permission to speak freely sir?"

"Granted,"

"Reverend Fairchild is a bigot who only agreed to work with me as Aaron and refused to acknowledge me in any other way." She shifted. "His third wife and I were good friends, and she was the one who helped me get off planet when she heard that the Governor had sided with Reverend Fairchild, who had turned me in."

"Then you identify as Female?"

"Yes sir," she was afraid, prepared for the dressing down that never came.

The captain simply nodded. "I will make sure your file is amended to properly reflect your preference. And I will remind the Governor that though that may be the way things work on the colony, that once you enlisted in the USL you became a galactic citizen capable of choosing your own identity. I will also make it clear that such treatment will not be tolerated, and that if necessary, the free ships might decide to re-negotiate their trade deals with them."

It might not be common to be transgender in the Girati, but it wasn't wrong, if you wanted to call yourself a wild Rovian, no one cared. You could just as well be a plant, and no one on the ship would blink twice.

"Thank you, sir."

"Is it Abigail or Abby?"

"When I'm on duty it is Abigail, when I'm off it's Abby."

The captain nodded. "Is that one reason you came here? To try and get away from that kind of past?"

"Yes sir and get away from Julian's family."

"Your husband?"

"Yes sir, he was—" She swallowed. "He was killed and the family blames me." She reached into her pocket and pulled out a picture. It was a wedding picture, her in a dress, and her husband in a tux. She held it out for the captain to see.

"We got sent to board a ship in the area and got ambushed. It's the same attack that got me my injury."

"Now that we have that awkwardness out of the way, Can I ask you about your injury?"

"They are calling it bio-morphic crystal. My chest and right arm are filled with small shards of it. And they have actually become part of skin, muscle or bone, so they cannot be removed. They don't often hurt, but so far we haven't found a way to stop them. The shards covered my husband entirely, he saved my life."

He could see the edges of purplish crystal under the fabric, glowing slightly. The whole thing put his teeth on edge, but he didn't know why.

"Has Jenna checked them out?"

"No, sir, the chief of security?" She was puzzled as to why she would need to.

"One, if they are bio-morphic I want to make sure they don't mess up BIOS, and two, you never know, she might be able to help you get rid of them as her implants are bio-morphic as well, so maybe she knows more about them." He smiled. "That is part of the reason she is here. With a unique understanding of the world, she may be able to tell us even more about them than the Doctor."

"I will speak with her. Thank you."

"You're welcome."

She stood a moment and was pleased that he didn't look at her in disgust. "May I ask a question?"

"Go ahead."

"How do you— I mean why are you—"

"Why am I ok with you being transgender? After all, Girati are some of the most culturally backwards there are?"

"I wouldn't have gone that far, sir, but yes."

"While we have very clear roles, they are not always defined by sex or gender. The reason that women are Mistresses is because it is their ability, our race shows an interesting biodiversity. Men don't have the same level of powers as women.

"So, the women move the ship, and the men protect them. So that they don't have to waste time or energy protecting themselves. Transgender among the Girati is not unheard of, just rare, because we really don't care which gender you identify with. One of my security chiefs was Agender," He shrugged. "They did their job well and that was all I could ask. I gave them a good recommendation when they left the ship. Last I heard they were married to a mistress and doing very well on Keltar.

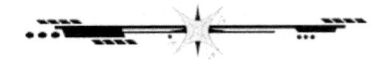

Jeffries lay in his bunk, unaware of the subterfuge about to be perpetrated in his name. He was a Sudec pilot, one of the best. He was always first on the rail and last on the line. He pushed harder and worked longer than anyone else. If he couldn't do it he didn't ask it of his men. He'd been paired with Abby. At first, he'd been an ass to her, but then he'd realized that, coming from the inner colonies, he'd lived too sheltered a life, and that he had to grow up. After he'd brought her favorite drink over and they'd shaken hands, the two of them were close. And when he'd lost his co-pilot to stimmshock, she'd volunteered.

They always had each others backs. And they both promised, no stimms, as tempting as the little gold energy pills were, they could really screw up your system. While they were legal, they were frowned on by most workplaces, but since they enhanced reflexes, they were often found on pilots who'd worked too many shifts. But it was easy, if you were exhausted, to overdose.

And what came after was Stimmshock, a condition that made your entire system go haywire. He was a personable, approachable pilot, and a hard worker. But like Abby, he had his own secrets. Some of them people knew but didn't talk about it. One of those open secrets is that his father had been a notorious slaver. He'd thought that would be a problem, since their Captain was Girati, but he just commented that he hoped the family stayed on the new path and kept going.

Twelve years ago, Stephen Jeffries had been one of the owners of the biggest slaver world in the Galaxy. He also was a reluctant participant. He didn't own enough to change things, but he didn't like the way his family ran what had been a legitimate business. Before the war and the OSU, what they had owned was a work camp, a place to work off your debts and start over. A man sentenced to work was treated well, paid well, and given room and board. And when his time was up, or he'd earned enough to pay back what was owed, he or she was free to leave. That was the way it was supposed to be, and that was the way young Jeffries wanted it to be. But in the years and decades that had passed, it had become true slavery, of every imaginable kind.

Which was how he had ended up stranded on Vega, outside the dome, and trapped. He was seventeen. He had twenty minutes of air and was a quarter of a light year from help. But the man he'd been working with, a tall, blonde-haired figure, had told him he wouldn't die. And without food or water, had managed to seal the suit and using only his own rebreather unit had hiked them two days out of the canyon where he had fallen.

That was after he had healed the wounds that had almost killed him. And the man, the one who had protected him and healed him, the one who had become his friend? He'd been one of the slaves assigned to him. And instead of using it to his own freedom, he got himself nearly killed trying to save a scared seventeen-year-old kid.

"You could have left me."

"Why, because you are your father's child?"

"Yes."

"And I'm mine. My father would have saved you and not for any other reason than he wouldn't be able to live with himself if he didn't. My father was a Girati, died when I was nine." He said as he tried to seal the break in the suit caused by the two stab wounds from the assassin.

"He didn't even live to see my blood mark. But everyone on my ship knew him, and his best friend was my godfather. That best friend's son became my best friend, and he would have saved you too. It's just what we are."

The two talked for hours, Jeffries about how he had never wanted to follow in his father's footsteps, and AJ about how he was old enough now to make his own decisions, and to turn the family back into what it was supposed to be.

"Your people weren't always slavers, most of the people who used to work, yeah, it was hard physical labor, but they were paid well and treated well, there to work off a sentence instead of rot in prison. And then someone got greedy and starting making up contracts. Going out and raiding. I can put you in touch with people who can help you clean out your ranks, make this job something to be proud of again. Secure your supply lines and keep the riffraff from coming back."

When they came back, the father gave his son whatever he wanted, so glad to have him back. And it ended up with Jefferies senior being arrested, AJ being released, with an emancipation mark, and Stephen working with the freer of slaves to set things right. After that, he put the empire in the hands of the most trusted of his men. Gave the freer of slaves authority to oversee and fled to the inner colonies to try to make himself a better man. AJ had passed his name to the recruiting office. And the office had tracked him down on Luna and offered him a billet. He took it.

As he lay there in his bunk, remembering all of this, and being glad that AJ had pulled him out of that crevasse, he began to feel tired, not just any tired though, the tired that came with being drugged, and he could taste chemicals. He had the presence of mind to activate his data recorder, a habit since the first time someone had tried to kill him. But quickly, darkness overcame him, and just before the world went entirely black, he saw a shadow move.

Conversations

Abby click-trilled quietly, timidly, hoping she got the pitch of the question right.

"I'm over here, hot-source."

Abby stood looking up at the Wraith, she clicked under her breath, a sort of apology for staring.

"What did you need?"

"It was suggested you might be able to help me."

"With what?"

Without a word, Abby unclasped her tunic and pulled it off to reveal the crystal across her shoulders and torso. "They call it bio-morphic crystal. From the little of your physiology, I understand it's like your implants."

"Exoskeleton." Jenna corrected.

"Pardon?"

"They are not foreign; they grow from my body. They are exoskeleton as systems start to fail the Grid-tech replaces them." She moved her metal fingers to show that they had grown from the nails. Jenna traced the line of the crystal with her fingers. "Does it hurt?"

Abby shivered. Sensation on the crystal was dulled, but the skin was cold, and the crystal didn't try to attack. It needed warm blood; it couldn't take the dead. And to the crystal, Wraith, being cold source, registered as dead.

"Much of the time, no, but if it gets hit or chipped at, yes. My body seems to be slowly changing. Except it doesn't respect bone and flesh unlike yours."

Jenna nodded. "Maybe we can re-engineer some of my nanites to reprocess it. Allow your body to adapt the crystal." When Jenna's hands left the edge of her breastbone, she buttoned her tunic back up.

"How did this happen?"

"My husband and I were investigating a ship. A crashed ship in the Delkari belt, a half a system-unit from my home world. The thing moved too fast, he pulled his weapon and shot, but the crystal shard embedded in his arm and started growing. The creature, for it was certainly no longer human, came at me and I pushed hard on the bulkhead and shoved it into the airlock and cycled it. I heard later that the creature was destroyed.

"But my husband reached up to touch me, and the crystal attacked me, it started over my left shoulder, and for the first two weeks I said nothing, but by the time I did it covered half my chest and my shoulder. When I started having pain, I reported it."

"Does it react to energy?" Jenna asked.

"Energy weapons hurt and make it grow faster." Abby affirmed.

Jenna nodded. "I don't know what it is, but I can work on it. Do you perhaps have a sample?"

"Here," A sample broke off easily under Abby's hand.

"Metal hand, not flesh, just in case." Jenna said as she reached out with her metal hand to take it. She had some suspicions that the thing could not use her since she was cold, but she didn't want to take a chance.

Jenna grabbed it with her black-hematite hand. And slipped it in a glass vial. "I will look at it later, but can I ask a more-personal question?"

"Of course?"

"How did the malfunction happen?" She gestured to Abby's form.

"Malfunction?" She was confused.

Jenna gestured to Abby's body again. "Your genetics say one, your program says another, which is correct?"

It took a moment for her to understand that Jenna was talking about her being genetically male. "Program?"

Jenna tapped her forehead. "Your program. Humans, Wraith we are all programmed. Yours, as much as I can read, anyway, says you are girl, but your DNA seems to not agree."

"I was born a male." Abby said.

"Ah, so your body was flawed. You are correcting it?" Jenna seemed to smile a little, though a true smile was hard for waith.

She nodded. That was a good explanation. "The doctor is helping me with Fourth Molt." Abby said. It was a term that many in space knew.

"Good. If no one was helping you I would have offered what help I can give." Jenna shrugged. "Though possibly not much."

"Do your people have fourth molt?" Abby was curious

Jenna click-trilled an explanation and then realized that Abby didn't understand. "Most of my people don't define gender. We may be genetically one or the other, but we don't-- interact as humans do, so, many of us have lovers of both sexes. And on occasion, we can have children, though that is becoming harder than it used to be, our genes are getting too narrow."

"Could your kind rewrite my DNA?" She frowned. "Make me as I'm supposed to be?"

"Is that what they say about us?" She shifted to sit, and then realized how tired her friend must be and shifted her hand, a stool appeared.

"I am sorry I forget that your body is more frail than mine."

She waited untilAbby had seated herself, "No, they probably talk about a grid-jack. We only do that if they are dying. It starts the process of being cold-source. But we can't do a lot with DNA, we fix by changing."

"So, your help?" Jenna nodded.

"Could kill you." Jenna held up her hand. "I have studied human biology and many other things, including genetics. As a cold source I wouldn't be able to help, but as warm-source, neither hot nor cold, maybe I can, I will speak with the doctor."

"Thank you." Abby said.

"Where did you learn Wraith?" Jenna asked.

"The computer."

"If you want to learn, I'd be happy to teach you. It's nice to have someone who wants to learn, and you can tell me about where you are from."

"Thank you, Jenna."

"You're welcome." She click-trilled a goodbye.

Strange

Even at three times the average speed of light, it was going to take nine days. Plenty of time for a shake-down. The captain had instituted hand-over-hand drills for the first two days after launch, just to knock the rust off, but he almost didn't notice the flash before the gravity changed and had to bounce hard to catch a handhold. He re-oriented to the 'feet- down' position and took a look both directions down the corridor.

The thing that had distracted him was the dream he'd had. Again. It was the little girl. The one that called him by his special name, the one reserved for those who knew him closely. Family and friends. But in two hundred years, he had made and lost a lot of those.

Lost in thought again, he found himself dropped unceremoniously to the floor when the gravity went back to normal. Most ships didn't do that, but then again, most ships didn't have Sudec, or rail guns either, most didn't have adaptive shields and Tucuran pilots.

But also, going into N-space without benefit of a stone, that was hard, one never knew what might happen, total gravity failure wasn't uncommon until the needles were properly adjusted.

But the other thing that had been weighing on him was the conversation he was going to have to have with AJ. The conversation he didn't want to have to have. And for now, it seemed like Fate was conspiring against him telling AJ, because almost as soon as he had shaken himself loose, and started walking to AJ's quarters, the comms paged him. He tapped the button on the wristband he wore.

"Go ahead"

"Sir, we need you down in Launch nine."

Tyrell found himself in front of a near mob. A ring of pilots on one side were being physically kept away from the two pilots under investigation. One lay on their back, and from where he was, he couldn't see the face. The flight suit was torn, and shards of purple crystal stuck out, the right arm was pinned entirely against her side, her eyes, open and blank, glowed purple, and the crystal had crept across her chest seeming to turn her chest and right arm down to the wrist into purple crystal. It had even climbed to her neck, making it all but impossible to talk, and making breathing hard.

Shards of crystal littered the floor between, people giving them a wide berth. A few of the crystals were dim and shattered at the slightest touch, the rest were still glowing slightly, trying to get back to their host.

As he carefully stepped forward, he drew in a breath. It was Abby. She lay on her back, barely breathing, and it was clear she had fallen, or jumped from the loading ramp. The Sudec sat on their tails, their open canopies twenty feet or more off the hard deck.

Nearby was Jeffries, who stood to one side, his mouth still hanging open a bit. It was clear he was bruised and battered, but he was upright. The surprise of falling or being pushed was still evident on his face. Though the pilot was good enough that there were immediate questions about how one or both of them came off the catwalk.

The doctor saw the captain and motioned him closer. "The crystal has grown, and I don't know what I can do to help her." He frowned. "I was helping her with her fourth molt."

He gestured to her body. Fourth molt was what Tucura called gender Transition. Since they molted three times, fourth molt was a concept they understood. "So I had scanned the crystals to see if there would be any issues, pain or otherwise. She had never seen them grow like this, and now her right arm is immobile."

He sighed. "She was talking a moment ago, but it hurts to talk now that they are impinging on her vocal cords."

"What about the other pilot?"

"She dropped him on the floor, but the crystals covered her, and she passed out before she could do anything more. She just kept saying something about 'its not right.'"

The captain walked over to Jeffries. Something about the young man was off, but he chalked it up to falling, or being pushed, off the walkway far above. The captain was always a good judge of body language. But right now, everything felt wrong.

"He fell off the gangway." He pointed up. "I had just touched the hatch to board. He said something and then next thing I knew he was throwing me off the gangway and a moment later, he followed." Jeffries explained.

Tyrell knew this was wrong. Jeffries and Abby were good friends, they had made it through training together. Maybe that was what she had been saying, not "Its wrong" but He's wrong.

As in something is wrong with Jefferies, as his best friend she would be the one to know.

"What's going to happen to him?"

"She's going to medical where she will be sedated until we can figure out how to help her."

"Good. He shouldn't be anywhere near the rest of us." Jeffries frowned. "His eyes went purple and he tossed me without even touching me. I thought psions were supposed to register so we all knew."

"She's not Psionic."

"Then he is now."

The captain walked over to the security officers. "Escort him to medical and have the doctor take a look at him, then, when he is done, take his statement, and remind the doctor that we humans get concussed easily..." he didn't want to tip his hand that he knew something was off, but it was.

"Ty," he could feel the long nails through his hair. "I thought you said you'd help me with the pins." His hands reached up to the fan of his wife's headdress and he pulled the pins that kept her hair up into the fan and helped her take the heavy headdress off.

Fortunately, this was ceremonial, much heavier than the clip she usually wore, so not something she had to wear all the time. With her hair down, it was as if the world shifted. The song quieted, almost into a buzz. She was off duty. One of the other ladies of the ship, probably Alis, would take her turn, and in this way, the ship stayed healthy. He could feel the ship moving beneath them, the plates thrumming in time with the engines, and in the back of his mind, the ship singing its own song of contentment; the crew was happy; the cargo was stowed, and they were on their way home for the first time in a decade, time to change crew and party, and take on supplies.

While Girati ships were mostly self-sufficient, there was only one time they were seriously vulnerable. Slowing to be ready for N-space. At that point they had only their small laser meant more for blasting asteroids, than ships, to defend themselves, and the fact that every Girati is trained in combat both in gravity and null. If they were boarded, they would take as many with them as they could.

The ship, as he remembered it, was beautiful, but the whole thing began to take on a purple cast. The lights became purple, the bands of light along the hall, the moiety line, all flowing, pulsing purple, and over it all, he could hear a voice.

"I could give them back to you. Let them dance with you forever."

"But there were some, who were bad." His wife started to turn purple. Not as if she weren't breathing, but into purple stone.

"You don't know? You don't understand? You don't remember? Tyrell? TY!"

He awoke with a start. His heart racing in his ears. "Nothing brings back the dead. Nothing," Tyrell told himself, mainly to quash that spark that demanded he ask the voice how, that he demand she do it. Whatever was brought back wouldn't be his wife, or his crew. They would Gahir, "Ghost children," the walkers called them "Those who followed back." Those who wouldn't go to the beyond, but tried to come back to life, stuck between.

Girati were superstitious, they had to be, and Rift Girati, the farthest out toward the rift in space where everything went strange, they were superstitious most of all. A year from help, out of reach of N Space? There was nothing but you and your crew and the steel and the stone. Nothing else between you and the black. They had been going home, and Tyrell had been meaning to meet them at Keltar. He'd had to leave the ship to solve an issue, he didn't know it was a trap. They had almost been back in range of N space. A few more hours and they could have jumped home. as they slowed down from rational in preparation for irrational, they were boarded without warning. The slavers didn't even bother with the warning. It was what the Girati called a "Blow and board" blow a hole and come on board from your ships before the sensors find you. If one is lucky, one swipes crew before they are mobilized.

His steel was known as free steel, and free steel has a tendency to draw free singers, those not bound to stay on a ship, and the spacers, pirates really, knew that. And so, they targeted the ship. And they had fought to the man. The ship he had come back to was nearly a ghost town. Nine hundred dead, one hundred and fifty injured. Many of them would never set foot on steel again, so bad were their injuries, they would retire to the station. Twenty-five missing and presumed lost. It sounded bad to non-Girati, but Girati taken as slaves were given a funeral. Most didn't last a year, if they were found later, they were given a '"re-awakening ceremony" that told the people they were alive, but even if they were, the odds were good they'd never serve again.

Being away from song and stone for too long tended to take their will to live. They became so dependent on the song and the others that being alone killed them.

He had helped wrap, remember, and space the dead. His ship had come back to Keltar, the home of all Girati, with only a handful of crew, and a captain so deep in despair they thought he might die. They put the ship away and sent him away to find his song again. Being around Keltar had been slowly killing him, and he worked his way through the galaxy from there. Only stopping when he had been arrested.

The Dream of the Walker

Toru kneeled in his quarters, backs of his hands to the top of his thighs, ankles crossed, eyes closed. He was at prayers, as usual this time of night, but something was off. It had been off since he'd set foot here. Shedda telepathy wasn't like most, it wasn't words it was images, emotions, and what he got, the flashes that disturbed his prayers scared him.

A field of statues, all made of red or purple stone, and the evil roiled off them in waves, a little girl, glowing purple eyes, a boy, holding her hand as if to calm her. And their eyes glowed purple, but she was-- he didn't know, but it seemed like the image of her wasn't real, or at least wasn't current. It felt like an old picture bent and frayed at the edges. Captain Tyrell, terrified, Bomb, the ship being torn to pieces. Bright light. Purple stone, a pilot, no, two of them.

AJ, on the floor, dead? Dying? He wasn't sure, but the picture came around again, The captain, panic, a bomb, the engine, the bomb, light, and then darkness. His eyes opened. The last two were a precognition. He knew it by the feel. There was or would be a bomb on the ship.

"Captain," Toru had come to the captain's ready room, knowing he would not be asleep. "You know that sometimes we see the future in our prayers."

Tyrell nodded and sat forward. He was a Girati, used to listening to the song of the Universe, and sometimes, it told you what could happen.

"It's a bomb, I couldn't see where it was, but the whole ship exploded in a flash as bright as the sun. There was no time to escape. Everything was gone."

The captain nodded. He would have asked if he was sure, but the look on Toru's face answered that question. It was sheer terror. It took a lot; he knew, to shake a Shedda. But the image and the feeling behind what he saw must have been bad to shake him like this.

"And the girl, she has something to do with everything, but not the bomb."

"I'll run a sweep, we know they are trying to destroy this ship before we can get our weapons systems all the way on line."

"Thank you, captain."

Captain's Log

CAPTAIN'S LOG, USLS 2019

    We picked up our first officer. We had to wait till after launch, and it seemed that no sooner had he arrived than we ended up in a royal pickle. We had to pick up my first officer, Toru, at Lexara station en route from Amara. Something happened, and he had been called home, and from what I understand that it is not a summons you ignore, so he met us nineteen hours in. It was, after all, supposed to be an easy cruise to the rim to get our needles for N space. And while N space didn't thrill me, neither did endless decades of travel. But things got off to an interesting start.

    Firstly, all of us in the command crew at least, are having nightmares, the same one. A little girl, a Girati girl, asking if we know her name, not sure who she is or what she means, if anything, counselor Kezen says she may just be anxiety about the new ship, but why are we all seeing it?

    After that, there was an attempted assassination. At least that's what I'm calling it. One of our SUDEC captains was thrown from the boarding catwalk by another pilot, one known to have a good sense of honor. And a pilot I'd had to speak with mainly because her record was wrong. She'd tossed him from the catwalk and fallen herself, aggravating an old injury. But that injury, biomorphic crystal, purple crystal—I don't know, somehow it sets ill with me, like I should know it, like I should understand what it means and why it is so dangerous.

Purple isn't a common color in space, so it's prized, and I can't think why this whole thing sets me ill at ease. There is something wrong but I can't place it. Maybe I've been off the steel too long, maybe I just don't know this crew well enough yet, but either way, something is seriously wrong.

I've sent the attacked pilot to be looked over and have his statement taken, while Abby, the pilot that threw him, is in the medical bay, unable to talk or move. She's been going in and out of consciousness for the past couple of hours, and so far, no one has any idea what to do about the crystal. And she kept saying that someone or something was wrong.

Toru came to me just before this all happened, telling me that there was a bomb on the ship, that he saw it in his prayers. Normally, I would be skeptical, but it takes a lot to scare a Shedda, and he was terrified. And maybe the fact that we can't find the bomb is what's setting me ill at ease.

Sabotage, Sabotage

The captain was still trying to puzzle it all out later that night. The sweep had come back clear, nothing identified as a bomb. But when he found it later, he would understand why. Everyone gave him their reports. Jeffries was being kept on watch, but one thing the captain did notice, Jeffries did not return to the barracks. While pilots were not required to, the team leaders usually spent most of their time with their men.

With a team leader in the medical, and her co-pilot acting odd, the captain knew something was wrong. And she expected him to return to the bay, maybe even take in the simulator, but he didn't he sat in the rec room and read, or played pool, or tried to find someone to lay bets on the next game. All things that he had never been known for.

Across the Rec room, AJ was glaring at him from his seat.

This this felt wrong. But the captain still didn't understand why it felt that way. It was during the next watch that everything started fitting into place. It all started with a seemingly random set of glitches in the lights. Nothing that was unusual considering this was a shakedown cruise.

A moment later, the entire ship lurched as she suddenly dropped out of FTL, and into regular space with the speed of a popped clutch. A second after, the main power failed for nine seconds. It didn't seem like long, but when main power came back on, it took almost ten minutes for diagnostics to finish. Bios had also gone offline with the main power. As soon as power was back on, it scanned again. This was what Bios was for. But it registered everything as clear.

The captain got two calls, nearly on top of each other. The first was from the weapons lockup.

"Captain, I was going through what we have and we are missing almost a pound of Kn-3."

Tyrell put down the hot coffee so he wouldn't be tempted to drop it. He knew what Kn-3 was but he asked just to be sure he had heard them. "High explosive?"

"Yes, sir, when power went off, the locks became manual. And someone popped it open and stole some. That's enough to blow two ships this size to kingdom come."

"And you're sure its missing?" Tyrell put his hands behind his back and paced. Something he did when he was worried.

"Log said we had 42.93 pounds of it. Now we have 42 even."

That worried the captain. An ounce was used in training. A pound? a pound would blow this ship and three more just like it out of space. How could almost a pound be missing?

"Condition critical!"

And that one thing, following his instinct and calling condition critical, saved his ship and forced the saboteur to out himself.

#

The doctor was the second call. "Captain, it's Abby." The doctor sounded like he was worried. "I swear it wasn't me."

Stevens said. "She's missing. When the lights went off she was here, and then there was a purple flash as she was gone. I don't know where she is, but the crystal has grown since she came in, and, sir, she doesn't read on Bios. I have her tagged temporarily, but I don't know how long that tag will last. The sedation didn't last. The stone seemed to tear it apart at the chemical level, so while I was doing blood work, I noticed something. Now, maybe they were trying to use it for an off-label treatment, but did you know she was on Imakura?"

He shook his head and then remembered he was on voice only. "No, why would she be on IM?" IM, as it was known in the outer rim, was dangerous and very expensive. Often smuggled in goods, it was something most Girati looked for in pure form. The drug was highly addictive. But it was also very good at making you remember things, true or not.

"I don't know. I know some people have a euphoric reaction to it, so maybe it was a high-dose painkiller, but one reason it's so hard to get a hold of is because it was first discovered by retrieval specialists. It can, under the right dose and circumstance shut down certain parts of the brain associated with memory, and it can activate others."

Tyrell nodded. "Specifically those dealing with truth and lie." He sighed. "See if you can tell me how long she's been on it," the captain said. "Do you have any idea where she went or why?"

"I just heard her say that something was wrong and then there was a flash and she was gone." He stopped to think a moment before replying. "Call me crazy but I think she went after the pilot she tossed off the boarding ramp earlier. She was upset that something was wrong with him and wasn't satisfied when he was allowed to leave earlier. I couldn't find anything to explain the sudden change in temperament, but he knew all the information from his history, just—slanted."

"Any chance he's altered? Been brainwashed?" Tyrell asked.

"Still running tests on that, and I'm also running a batch process on his DNA make sure we aren't dealing with a chimeric or a sleeper. "

"If he's a chimeric shifter then he may know the person's history, but he can't change his own temperament."

Stevens sighed "That is true, but if you would allow me to follow my mother's people, my instinct says he's a clone." Tucura didn't often allow leaps of faith or instinct. "He's probably a fast grow. That means, at most we have a week to find him."

"What makes you say that?"

"Shift in temperament was too fast, if it were chemical there would more chance of the actual person coming through, but this is solid, there is no fight in his mind. He knows who he believes himself to be."

"But the other reason is that it gives us hope." The doctor half-smiled, "If he's a quick grow, that means that there is a good chance our pilot is alive."

Security

"Security Alert!" The captain called. "Re-run BIOS."

"We are still reading everyone accounted for." Jenna replied.

"Wait." Something nagged at him. "Doc said that Abby didn't register on bios, so subtract her life sign and re-scan."

"All accounted for." Jenna's all-whisper sounded confused.

"How can we have all the crew if I just told it we were missing crew?" The captain asked.

"That means someone is reading twice. So where is our pilot?" Jenna hit the buttons to try and figure out why someone was reading twice. "This is strange."

"What?" Tyrell snapped. He was getting a headache.

"I'm reading—I don't know what I'm reading, it's like a phantom signal. Not broadcasting as if alive, and not always there, but it's just often enough to hit the BIOS scans." She made the gesture of confusion.

"What do you mean?"

Jenna thought for a moment. How might a human trick BIOS? "I think someone built a resonator that only broadcasts life signs when Bios scans, otherwise its dormant, so when Internal sensors scan, they get nothing, but BIOS can still ping it. And since BIOS overrules, it marks him as here."

"Its double-counting Jeffries?" Tyrell's headache was suddenly much worse.

"It looks that way, but I can't get a lock on where it is, BIOS only tells us who, without being able to lock with internal scanners, it won't tell me where." Jenna frowned. "I will have to work on it so this will not happen again.

"So, someone has cloaked him while this imposter took his place," Tyrell said. It was the only thing that made sense. Wherever he was, BIOS was still scanning him. "Scan for Jeffries, also scan for any small ships, or anyone attempting to launch. Also see what you can do to find some way to get scanners to lock on to our other Jeffries signal. I want my crewman back."

Tyrell touched the crystal around his neck "And where is Abby?"

"I have her tag in hanger maintenance bay one; she's not moving."

"Ok, keep an eye on her, tell me if she moves." He sent a prayer to Ona.

The second version of pilot Stephen Jefferies slid out from between the deck plates, shedding his breather as he did. Carefully he reattached the plate. He had only a few minutes before the scan registered him as being somewhere he shouldn't be. It didn't take long to sabotage the scanner on the core, a couple of twisted wires and it looked like an installation error. The freak on the bridge couldn't fix it. They'd have to fix it by hand.

It took just about as long to place the mine at the base of the engine, inside the housing. It couldn't be seen unless someone shimmied under the panel, and no one paid any attention to a gray shirt shimmying under a panel in engineering. They figured he was checking something. In a week or two, when everyone knew everyone, he wouldn't have been able to pull this off, but now, when people were just people, he could.

He had connected it and set the timer before shimmying out of the core. "We were having a little bit of trouble with the relay," he said as he shimmied out again. "Should be fine now." He walked back out of engineering before anyone asked.

No one had a chance to question before BIOS gave them another mystery. Abby was missing, one moment she had been there, and the next, she was gone in a flash of purple light. Of course, no one knew that the purple light wasn't from a ship or protocol.

"Scan for her, look for the doctor's tag," the captain said. "Jenna expand our scan to the outside of the ship, look for any small ships close enough to transport through our hull." He raised a hand. "I know it's unlikely, but it's more likely than they just vanished."

"Captain, we're reading a hard launch sequence has been started on one of the SUDEC."

"Whose?"

"Jeffries. He's trying to launch. Rail control has been locked. He can't leave."

AJ

"AJ." The girl sat alone under the trees in hydroponics, picking grass leaves idly. "You could never be happy serving under the man who killed your wife." The little voice said.

"Go away." He threw a blade of grass at her.

He knew he was dreaming. He hadn't been here under the trees in years. And the vibration of the ship was wrong. His hand reached out to touch the bulkhead. "This is just a dream."

"But it can be real." The voice said. The girl who appeared was out of focus, he couldn't see her features.

"No, it can't go away." He frowned. "Free singers shouldn't marry bound singers." He turned away from the child.

That was what it had boiled down to. Alis was a bound singer. She could not leave the ship. Not without getting weak and possibly dying. But his otherness made their stone wary. The stone didn't like him, didn't want him, and did everything to force him off the ship. When it became a matter of security of the ship, he had resigned as head engineer and got off at the next port of call. He didn't see Tyrell again for years. Not until they both rotated onto the same freighter.

"You forgot me." The petulant cry broke him out of his memory.

"Are you still here?" He turned back to the child.

"Why are you being so rude?" She pouted. "That's not at all like hospitable Girati."

"You are just a dream. Just a memory of a song. You can no more bring back the dead than I can, so I ask, in the memory of my wife, to go away and stop bothering me."

Now the girl was angry. Her eyes flashed purple, something AJ didn't like. "You will pay, you will all pay."

AJ didn't like the sound of that, and somewhere in the back of his head was the memory of what she was, and then there was pain and blackness. The bed he'd been sitting on came up to meet him quickly and he knew nothing more for hours.

"Ne-kishe Aja." AJ shouted as he jumped the pilot. He didn't remember getting there. In fact, the last thing he remembered was the dream. But he knew one thing: this man was not the man he had made his brother. This man was not family.

The first blow landed hard and carried them both to the deck, as the pilot, stopped from leaving the ship, had returned to rec room to think. "You are not my brother."

The words would have sent shivers through any of the Girati on the ship, but Jeffries just tried to avoid him. This angered AJ even more. "You are not my Brother! You do not deserve that name. I know your Hidden name. I know the name that you do not speak."

What had started as an ambush quickly became a brawl, but those looking on later would realize that something was seriously wrong. AJ and Jeffries had fought before. It happened, usually when one or both were drunk, but now, AJ was winning, but it wasn't the winning between friends, it was the "He's black ops and Jeffries isn't" kind of win. Even pulling his blows so he didn't kill him, AJ was wiping the floor with him, a man who had learned to fight before he learned to speak. He was wiping the floor with a man he had seen kill an assassin in one sure stroke without flinching or hesitation. He was a man who knew almost as many ways to kill a man as he did. The two were normally evenly matched.

But during the fight, AJ didn't hear the hiss of the spray. He didn't really feel the prick of the needle, but either way, the battle suddenly turned as security came and broke them up.

By then AJ looked drunk, though the barkeep swore he hadn't had anything but coffee. And he could barely keep his feet, and the other man was bloody and playing the victim card. "Ne-Kish Aja" AJ muttered, but as the time went on, he began to realize something. It was getting harder and harder to think. "Call the captain. Must talk to Tyrell."

For the second time in as many hours, the floor came up to meet AJ abruptly, and he knew no more. When he awoke a little later, he knew something was wrong. Already half his language was gone, and the place on his shoulder where he'd been given the shot was on fire. His arm was red and tender.

He was in the brig, not a surprise really, but his brain was going back and forth between knowing what a brig was and not being able to tolerate it, let alone understand being confined. For Girati to be confined against their will for anything but quarantine was unusual. But he felt drunk, except his head was getting cloudier, not unclouded.

Double Trouble

"Captain, it's not him." He repeated.

AJ put his head against the table. He'd ended up in a cell because he'd been fighting with the pilot from earlier. Stephen Jeffries. The words were slow and strained, as if he couldn't remember. Terror filled his eyes as his ability to speak Standard left. He knew this feeling and he didn't like it. He got up and paced, trying to force some semblance of normalcy to his features, any syllable of Standard from his lips, and any steady motion from his body.

On top of that, it was hard for him to stand straight. He felt like the ship was swaying side to side, his eyes bloodshot, and his vision dim. He knew what this was. Finally, he sat. He took a deep breath, laying his cheek against the cold metal of the table. He was feverish. Whatever Jeffries had given him, he'd had it before, but the name was lost to him. Jeffries was in another cell and as he talked, AJ became more and more frustrated and agitated, gesturing to the young man. Finally, he spoke again, this time in Girati.

"Aja Intari Aja," he said quietly, not lifting his head, "Yenam, Tejan."

He was beginning to get frustrated as he couldn't switch languages. He put his head up frowning. He was not thinking in the same language he was speaking; he had reverted to Girati. "Te Stena sell te bel Lir a non."

It was the highest oath of a Girati, "The stone will be silent, the blood will lie, if this is untrue.

"AJ?" Tyrell asked.

AJ just shook his head and got up. He paced for a moment, terror in his eyes before he spoke again, kneeling next to the captain.

"Fe'an, Tejarih, Ruka." His hands clasped for the Captain's sleeve, hands scrabbling to try and find the words he needed, but thinking in standard and speaking in Girati was hard.

"Get him sedated," the captain said, a hand running through AJ's hair. "Shur," he shushed him like a child having a bad dream.

That terror was still there. "Shur nam ket."

"Shh," the captain said as the doctor moved behind AJ. AJ tried to twist away but the compound the doctor gave him acted immediately. "Bring him to Medical, put him in stasis. I have to check something out. We're gonna get hailed, probably by a ship calling itself Blackbird, and when they call, patch it through to me."

"Yes, sir."

The captain walked out of the cell and stopped in front of the one across the hall. He turned to the guards.

"Unclip the pilot's gloves and push up his right sleeve."

"Sir?" the guard said, not understanding what the man was doing. It wasn't against the rules, but they didn't know enough Girati custom or law to understand.

"I'm looking for something." Tyrell replied.

The guard did so and there was a small red mark, about a half inch long.

"He was right." The captain said. "This isn't our pilot."

"How do you know?" The guard asked.

"He should have an Ajari." The captain rolled up his own sleeve to show the mark in the same place, though his was a white scar that was slightly raised. "One of the few things we intend to scar." He nodded towards the pilot. "That's an attempt at an Ajari by someone who has never seen one."

"Isn't that a blooding mark?" the security officer asked.

The captain nodded. "AJ has two. He told me a couple years ago, he'd taken another to save someone's life. His healing ability only works on family, so he made the boy family to save his life. Besides, the kid had already saved his life."

"So the real one would have this—Ajari?"

"Yeah, it should look like mine." Tyrell sighed. "That's what AJ kept saying. That he wasn't family. That he didn't know him, and that he didn't answer to his hidden name."

The doctor had come out of Aj's cell with the young man on a stretcher. He stopped in front of the captain to speak a moment. "When are you going to wake AJ up?"

"When Blackbird calls. He can't speak Standard, I've seen this once and last time it nearly killed him."

Tyrell turned back to the guard. "Keep an eye on our imposter, don't let him out of your sight. Warn me if anything changes."

Tyrell walked out of the brig and down the hall.

"Security." The voice comms was working, fortunately, and so he was connected to the bridge station.

"Yes, sir," Jenna's soft musical many-voice spoke.

"Exclude our prisoner from BIOS as long as he remains in the cell. We have an imposter. Remain at Critical. All crew are to remain in quarters until further notice. Those at duty stations are to stay there until we've had a chance to sweep. And have a conversation with BIOS and find out how they fooled it. I want to find the real Jeffries."

"Aye, sir." she responded.

He hit the buttons to change channels "Doc, how's AJ?" He knew the doc would have gotten him to the med bay by now

"He's in stasis, but he just keeps saying the same phrase over again. Pardon my words if I misspeak them. 'Fe'an, Tejirah Ruka.' The Translator is stumped I just know he's telling you to do something." The Tucuran snorted, something he did when irritated. "He made me promise."

"Girati doesn't have a word for the Grim Reaper. So we used an old one for Graveyard. He's asking for the Avengers. And they are probably on their way." The captain sighed. "I'm not cleared to say a lot about it except he worked with them for a while, and was allowed to leave because he had medical issues."

Later, much later, the captain would realize how distracted he was. His best friend was in stasis, but he didn't immediately check the history. He didn't know why, he thought this was just a flashback from the mission that had nearly killed him. If he had known at this time what he learned later, he might have solved the mystery much sooner.

"Captain, this is engineering." The voice of Sampson was annoyed. "I found out how they got into Engineering without us noticing. You really should come see this."

The captain walked in and stopped cold. The hull plates had been taken up and underneath between the primary and secondary hull was a gap and this gap, usually used only for wiring and components, had been filled with a container. It was a bio-unit.

"It's shielded against our scans. Dating puts it back to before the ship held Atmo. Our imposter didn't get into the ship, he was built here. Fast-acting, short life clone. According to what we see here he's got another two days before he drops dead. So, two days to blow us out of the sky."

He pointed to the housing of the engine. "Mos' the program was done from inside the bio-unit. An' the explosive ain't missing. The logs was tampered with. This device was built into the housing for the core before we ever launched. The hull plates here are on a repulsor. He clicked a key an' the whole thing opened for him, and the lights and BIOS went out. I'd wager that it didn't happen until our pilot was out of commission. If we are lucky, the pilot is unharmed. It looks like he was supposed to climb back in his bio pod before shutdown and we'd never be the wiser. The other pilot goes about his business, an' when everything went to hell, he takes the blame. 'Cept the other pilot pushed him off the boarding path."

"So, was she trying to save us? Did she have a premonition?"

"I dunno, but there's a lot of that going round. A girl who keeps asking a question we can't answer. An' I feel like I should know her. Like her name is one I know, like I've heard of her somewhere, but I can't think of where."

Getting out of his cell was easy. He just used the override that was built into the system. The override disabled the ability of the scanners to track him and gave him about a five-minute head start before anyone would be able to find him.

First thing was he had to find that creature that had pushed him off the boarding rail. The thing had tried to stop him. It had tried to protect the ship. Talking to him as if he would ever befriend a creature like that... As if he would ever turn against the true humans. The chronometer was counting steadily; he didn't have long. In a matter of a day, he'd be dead and this ship would be gone. And the OSU will have won the war, and could go back to making humanity safe from all the outsiders, the ones pretending to be human who would take their jobs, and hurt their people. Look at the pilot. He had thrown him hard without touching him. Psion freaks were supposed to be catalogued, so they didn't hurt people. Instead, the captain had sided with it.

It didn't matter if he was Nameless; he had tried to go against the Union, so he had to die. Besides, turning into a psionic creature, he'd rather die. Of course, this Jeffries didn't know his other self had much different views, having been programmed to believe this way in the tank, he came out believing that the one true leader of the union was Captain Rican. That the only true humans were a slim set of base codes of DNA. He was a walking, talking propaganda guide for the OSU and the purity patrols they spawned. Psions and others were considered non-human. Of course, the irony was, so was he. He was as inhuman as it came; he existed only to die. Barely self-aware, he was a quick-grow clone, born knowing how long he would live, and never more than seven days. But a clone could do a lot in seven days, like end a war or start one. All this went through his head as he dodged officers and made his way to Medical.

Captain's Log

CAPTAIN'S LOG, SUPPLEMENTAL....

AJ is in medical suffering from a drug or flashback I've only seen once. Last time this happened, it nearly killed him. I'm expecting to be contacted by the Avengers soon because of this. He couldn't speak Standard, and he could barely stay on his feet. If I didn't know better, I'd say he was drunk, but the barkeep swore nothing stronger than coffee. AJ doesn't drink much; a single drink can send him into fits, with his Resan metabolism. He still looks bad, but yesterday, he couldn't speak anything but deep rim, and could barely keep his feet. But the thing he kept telling me was that our second pilot, the one pushed off the catwalk, wasn't our pilot. The real one, it turns out, should have an Ajara, a blooding mark on his arm, but the one that the imposter has is made by someone who has never seen one.

Now our pilot is missing. And the dreams are still there. It isn't about the ship, not directly anyway, it's about someone and I don't know who, but she seems familiar.

The Real Man

IT HAD BEEN HOURS since AJ had been put in stasis. The scan was proceeding for the missing crewman. Living or dead, BIOS should have been able to find him. It might not, except that one of the pilots had been caught in the barracks when the order came. So he went back to his bunk, surprised to see Jeffries, the top bunk sleeper, dead asleep on his bunk. Something sat on his chest making a silver sheen over him. The young man reached out to check pulse since the scanner wasn't working and the device sparked and died, leaving a sleeping man on his bunk. BIOS was finally able to lock on and his call came about the time that BIOS pinged.

"Captain, this is Lieutenant Sanders, I think I found Jeffries, he's on his bunk."

"Upload initiated" the computer said.

"What's going on?"

"He had a data recorder it seems that triggering the shield triggered the upload. At first glance it seems to be his vitals and position for the past seventy-two hours."

"Is it on auto-upload?"

"Yes."

"Good. Stand by. I'll send the doctor to check him out and we can make sure he isn't hurt."

Not only did the data recorder give them valuable information about his medical condition, it proved, without a doubt, that he was not the man who had been pushed off the catwalk. Besides the lack of injury, there was no way he could be both asleep and fighting with Abby.

The one thing no one could explain was the image of someone, or something, that had been on the tape for just a moment, for no more than a couple of frames at the end. This figure seemed to have no face. He was just solid black, but in his hand what looked like a vial of poison or sedative, and a moment later, the figure was gone.

Once an Avenger

AT THE OTHER END of the galaxy, the team that had rescued the ship from crashing on Terra were getting a notice that one of their team members was in trouble. AJ had been an Avenger, once upon a time, but an attack had sidelined him, and now, that same issue was cropping up again.

"Major?" It was the team's Doctor. "I'm getting a Transceiver squeal on one of our members who isn't active. AJ."

"What type of squeal?" Major Hunter, or as his handle was "the grim Reaper," asked.

Cyborg, their doctor, was looking over the reports with a frown on his face. "He's in stasis, scanners are showing some sort of distress, pretty similar to what took him off active duty. He needs the antidote and most doctors have never seen this stuff let alone treated it."

"Whip up the antidote and come with us." Reaper said.

"All due respect sir, you're going to have to take one of the other doctors." The towhead frowned. "I'm banned from the ship, it's in my own time stream." He sighed. "I know, I know, we don't talk about time and dimension, except one of my younger selves is on that ship.. or will be."

"Wait, you're on the ship?" He tried to remember the future history of this particular young man, but he blanked on this part.

The younger man nodded. "Not yet, I will be, and I can't afford to make the captain biased for or against me. He's never met the younger me. He doesn't know what is going on and if we bias him I may never end up on the crew."

It was always interesting when they ran into their own timeline. Even Mike had to be careful. He had multiple doubles here. Fortunately only one was aware of Major Hunter, the others weren't, they'd never met, but it was still strange watching yourself and understanding instantly what was going on. Of course, it was always more interesting when he didn't understand. Mike didn't live life in order anymore, hadn't for a long time. So sometimes he met his future self before his future self met his past self... It was hard to explain, and way off topic, so he pulled his mind back to the present.

"If you see yourself, no you didn't," reaper said, reminding himself of the rule of time travel.

"Pix, find him, let's get ourselves ready."

tick tick tick

DISARMING A BOMB ATTACHED to the core was hard. Doing it without disrupting power or getting fried was even harder. And the padding meant to protect you was far too bulky to fit into the crawlspace. The bomb was simple. The device itself had been built into the casing, and the Saboteur just needed to add the arming device and the whole thing was live. The problem was, without the arming device, which the pilot had, trying to disarm it was hard.

Jenna was running code from her seat trying to find a way to unravel its computer, but the code was solid. Almost too solid. Two ensigns were on their backs underneath the panel trying to save the ship from imminent destruction, but working under the core was hot and hard, and they only had ten minutes to avert disaster.

"Jeffries's doppelganger is here and just armed the bomb, Captain, but we are working to disarm it."

None of the security officers could fire, an energy discharge this close to the core could be disastrous. He ran up and down hallways seemingly at random, and doubled back when he could, but eventually they figured out where he was headed. He was headed for Medical to kill AJ and the pilot.

"He's headed to medical and not appearing on the scanner."

The officer said, "He's half deck ahead of us and has turned some of the security protocols against us."

"Keep track of him."

As he entered, he made his way for AJ, but what happened was much faster than it would take to say it. The doctor was ready with a sedative, but as he approached, the figure on the slab, now more stone than woman rose, and touched the doppelganger. All of the people nearby were pushed back roughly as her hand connected with the chest of the imposter. It seemed just a moment and crystal engulfed the figure, too. It covered him in the space of two or three breaths, and then the killer, once known as Abby stepped over him and disappeared in a flash of purple light.

A few seconds later, before anyone knew what was happening, Abby was pulling one of the gray shirts from under the console and reaching in with her hands. Impossibly, she was strong enough to rip the bomb free of the housing and pulled it to her chest where it attached.

"Cannot let them kill us," she muttered, and in a wash of purple light, she was gone and the bomb with her.

They scanned the ship for her but couldn't find her. Then the captain thought about it and expanded the search to the outside, and sure enough, she was floating in space, now a ball of crystal glowing and pulsing.

"Captain we don't have long." The ensign said as the numbers on the screen began to climb.

"Back us up, shields, brace!"

"We are receiving communication." It was the ensign at communication.

"From whom?"

"it's Abby." He paused, realizing he had called her by first name instead of her rank, but the captain just gestured what he took to be absolution.

"On speaker."

"I cannot let them take me. I cannot become nameless, you must stop them, remember what you have forgotten." The voice was no longer human. It was modulated-- no, it was many voices. A sound he had heard before long ago. It was the sound of a Stone having taken over a human.

There was no warning when the crystal blew, just a bright pinpoint of light and the comm was dead. "Nothing but crystal shards, sir, should we pull them in?"

"No, they are far too dangerous for that." The response was automatic. If this was a stone trying to regrow itself, then even one shard could be dangerous.

Tyrell stood there in shock. Then he found himself seated in his chair. For a moment the memory of waves of grief and fear washed over him as he remembered his own ship dying all those years ago.

One of the young men on the bridge, he wasn't sure who, handed him a cup of hot coffee, and he instinctively took a sip. It seemed to settle his nerves a bit, something he knew, something common.

A hand landed on his back. "This was her path, Captain. You cannot blame yourself. But nor can you live in the memory of sadness." Joru said. "Keep walking." the last two words were a near whisper. meant only for him. "Keep walking,' keep living, keep moving. Don't stop to wallow.

Tyrell took another sip of his coffee and cleared his head.

The Planet

"Captain, I wouldn't have noticed it, except I was recalibrating sensors after the blast... there's a planet in this system with faint life readings."

"I wouldn't go there," Jenna's voice whispered.

"Something wrong?" The captain turned to the Wraith.

"I'm reading more of the stone, and—something else, I don't know what, but I don't have a good feeling." She made an all-encompassing gesture and a click that just meant 'wrong.'

The sensor tech turned and started pushing buttons; if she said there was something there, there was something there. "Scanning. There is evidence of some sort of base. I have cloaking satellites and communication relays all systems broadcasting on OSU bands."

"Fully automated sir." The young man said. "no signs of life. But it is giving us a name N1M31355."

"Looks like we found an outpost." Tyrell said. Now he knew where the patches had come from.

"Back us off, we don't want to trip the security system."

"Aye, Captain." Backing off. Conn made the adjustments to a safer distance.

"Captain, I'm reading ion disturbances of at least three ships, and there is evidence of two more in the debris here. It appears there was a battle here within the past few hours." As they had moved, more of the area around the station came into scanner range, and they were able to get more information.

"Scan for survivors." He took a sip of the coffee still in his hands. For a moment, everything was right with the universe, and he hoped that the death of his crewman would mean that the rest of the mission would be good. "Give me that for her, please."

"I have a single life sign among the debris. Its a shuttle, one lifeform aboard, but the signal is—distorted I can't tell what type of life sign."

The first shot seemed to come from nowhere. It rocked the ship and destroyed some of the debris. To have timed the shot for that close when traveling through n-space, was difficult.

"Ship just emerged from N space, they are locked on us. Firing again."

The second blast shook the ship.

"No damage." The young man at the sensors replied. "Low yield. Just trying to get our attention."

The captain opened his stance against further rocking. "Scramble the fighters. Come around and put a spike across their bow. Don't chip the paint, but make them take note."

"Aye sir, coming around. CQWS are online, target is hot." This voice was behind the captain at the weapons systems.

"They are firing." Weapons said nothing that the other ship had beat them to the fire.

"No damage again."

The ship lurched as they fired the rail guns. A single shot skimmed across the other ship's shields, throwing fireworks before it exploded close enough to shake their ship to its core.

"Being hailed." communications said.

"This is the OSU ship Black Star; you have fired on us unprovoked, stand to and prepare to be boarded."

"This is The USLS 2019, even if that were true, we don't recognize your authority outside the Earth system and the standard SOL orbit. You fired on us first, so we returned the favor. Stand down, power down, and prepared to be towed."

"Captain, I'm reading a strange energy build up coming from the other ship."

"Go Captain, run before you meet our fate." The multi-voice was suddenly replacing the voice of the other captain. "You cannot run from the Nameless."

"Captain," Jenna's voice was concerned. "The life signs are disappearing. And there is that--" she made the same sign as before. "Thing again."

"Go captain, before she takes you too. It's too late, go." The captain of the Black Star fought through the crystal and lunged for the main control.

"Engines critical." Sensors said, trying to keep the fear out of his voice.

"Brace!" The captain said. "Shields." He reached for the comms "Brace for impact!"

Those who could, grabbed for the closest thing they had, and as the ship in front of them exploded, the wake washed over them.

The loaded rails locked down so that the ship couldn't fire as it was rocked by shockwaves.

Slowly the shaking stopped, and the screen came back online. "Minor damage, deck ten, launcher three is damaged, CQWS are still functional, slight drop in targeting accuracy. "

"All stop." Tyrell said pulling himself off the deck. He shifted to make sure he wasn't hurt. "Anyone hurt?"

The bridge crew all answered negative, no one was hurt, just shaken and bruised. "Recalibrate sensors and give me a sweep. Tell me where the escape pod is."

"Captain, still a life sign in the debris, but there are no survivors from the Black Star. They went down with all hands, no escape pods."

The captain stood for a moment. He had seen devotion like that. He had seen the crew fight to the man to save the ship. But an OSU ship? That honorable? Was this really virtue, the crew fighting to save the others, or was this a captain's fear, pride and vanity? What spurred such a violent reaction? Captains didn't destroy their ships often, and especially not with all hands aboard. And the fact that there were no escape pods told him this wasn't the crew, this was a captain's fear. Something had scared the captain enough that he would destroy his own ship, and himself, to be rid of it. Whatever that stone was, it had scared the captain enough to scuttle his own ship without warning.

They had completed most of an orbit of the station before the captain heard the trill that brought his attention. "What do we have?"

"Small run-about to port." Security said. "Minimal weapons, and shields are weak. It's being fired on by a Takarev class destroyer that just came from the planet's cloaking field. I must admit I am unfamiliar with that one captain, and the database still has limited information."

"Fortune favors us." The captain said with a smile. "I know a little about their newest class of ship. It's what this ship used to be."

"So similar weapons and armament."

"No, similar hull plating and sensors, our weapons systems were loaned to us by the Tucuran, our nasty little fish-faces down on deck ten are here to see how they perform. Our shields are also new, absorption matrix."

"Then what are the standard weapons?"

"General band-lasers," the captain said. "If this were a heavy cruiser we were up against, we might be in trouble. Open a channel to the ship in distress. "

"Channel open."

"Unknown ship, this is the USL-- 2019, we have heard your distress call."

"This is the runabout Garnet, My name—my designation is K101. I claim political asylum under the rules of the USL having been kept beyond my appointed term and being made known that there is no hope of release, only death."

"Captain, we don't have time for this, they get any more direct hits and he won't live long enough to come on board." the young man at the scanner cut off what he knew would be a long conversion just by the fact this was a unit.

The captain nodded that he wanted to hail the ship. "We've accepted your proposal, hold for transit. We will send a crew down to protect you, K101."

"Open a channel to the attacking ship." Tyrell said.

"We're being ignored."

"General quarters, pilots to bays, Close Quarters Weapons Online," the captain ordered.

"CQWS are hot, targeting up. We are getting all green," Jenna said in her musical whisper. "Bays 1, 2, 4 and 7 are hot sir." She elaborated.

"I thought we were supposed to have eight bays." The captain said.

"The others still haven't been finished." She said.

"One and seven are Port?" Tyrell was trying to remember the way the rails were set up, he half-closed his eyes doing the math in his head.

"Yes sir, evens starboard, odds to port." Jenna said.

"Extend the port side launchers. Starboard thrusters, station keeping, prepare to launch." One had to remember that the rails were on one side or the other, so if you were only firing one side, you had to use thrusters to keep position or you would flip the ship over. Not really a problem except for targeting computers.

"Squadron one, I need you there protecting the ship; bring him on board in one piece." Tyrell said as he wished the small craft pilots well.

"Aye, sir." He heard the whole squadron answer together.

"Launch when ready," the captain said, turning over control of the launch to the rails. The ship shimmied a little as seven small versions of their ship flew out. Each fighter could be rail launched, and carried a complement of small lasers and a single rail gun.

The captain got up and paced. "All right, still ignoring the hail?"

"Yes sir. They have noticed us." Security said, "And the definitely noticed the ships. They are locked on."

"The ships can take care of themselves, but I feel like the ugly girl at the party," the captain said.

"They are attempting to scan us again."

"Good, let's give them something to talk about. Put a shot over their bow, same as last time. Let's make them sit up and take notice."

"Aye, sir. Targeting space just outside their shields." The voice behind him was calm and it seemed to help keep him calm.

"Fire."

A solid projectile hurled at just under the speed of light was an awesome thing to watch on sensor. At the distance they were aiming, it should blow past them and detonate harmlessly. But the wake alone was enough to give the gravity systems fits. Moments later, there was an answer to their hail.

"This is Patrol ship Reston, your ship has fired on us without provocation. Your ship is forfeit, stand to and prepare to be boarded." The captain stood, soot marked, bloody, hands behind his back attempting to project an air of menace, but it was clear his ship was in a bad way.

"This is Captain Tyrell of the USL 2019, you have no jurisdiction off Terran obit, by section nineteen of the treaty signed last year."

"You are in our way." The captain said

"There is a small ship that you are firing on, the pilot of which, is under our protection." Tyrell said. "Stand down."

"That thing belongs to us."

"The ship?" Tyrell asked. He was sure what the answer would be, but he felt like the crew needed to be reminded the stakes.

"The UNIT." The captain said. "Its ours and we will have it back."

"The gentleman is no one's property. He has claimed asylum under USL Law, you have thirty seconds to stand down or we declare your vessel hostile."

The OSU captain snorted. "You think because you stole one of our ships you are a pilot?" He laughed. " Girati, go play trader somewhere else. How could you think that you could approach us?"

Tyrell just shook his head. "Check your sensor logs; what we have you can't hope to match." The captain said with a smile. "I'd rethink your stance.

"They are sending Rally Point. Attempting to jam." Comms said.

Rally point was a call for backup. There was a long, tense silence. "I jammed it, but I don't know how much of the message got through."

"All right, target propulsion and weapons," the captain ordered before turning to his adversary on screen.

"Time's up. Your ship is hostile," Tyrell said. He, too, had his hands behind his back, but he looked unruffled and he walked softly. He smiled at the other captain, a rather wolfish smile. "So here is what is going to happen, we are going to take out your propulsion systems and your weapons and leave you here while we go about our business."

"They are charging weapons."

"Absorption shield to maximum." Tyrell said, with the air of a man ordering coffee. No urgency, just statement.

The enemy ship fired, lasers lancing off the shields and then scattering over the entire ship as the shields translated the energy into useable energy and stored it. "System stable, entire blast has been absorbed. Should I remodulate it back at them?" Weapons asked, hand hovering over the button.

"No, let's leave that card for a while. Never good to show your entire hand on the first play." He smiled. "We warned them, take out propulsion and weapons. Aim for non-personnel areas if you can." The spikes fired at sub light speed could tear through the ships like paper, and none of the others had seen this system yet, so he targeted places where loss of life was minimal, but the ship would be disabled. He wasn't always going to be so kind, but right now he saw no reason to destroy them.

"Aye, sir." weapons said, pressing the keys to do as the captain said.

Again, there were thumps as the CQWS spun up to launch.

"Direct hit, they are dead in the water." So far, they were only using the smaller rails. The main one hadn't been finished yet, and when it was, even a heavy destroyer wouldn't be much of a problem.

"SUDEC hailing, captain." Communication replied as he patched the call through.

"This is Squadron one, we are in sphere formation, the ship is protected, heading for the bay."

"Copy that."

The small sphere of ships, their absorption shields linked in a sphere, had surrounded the tiny ship. It was flying back under guard. Once it was within range of the bay, they broke off and formed a staggered line out front.

"Sir, the—" Jenna made the sign again. The one he was starting to hate.

"Shields!"

Before anything else could be said, the ship blossomed into a bright point of light.

"The ship has self-destructed." the young man at the sensor said. His voice was low and flat, to see one ship go like that was hard, but three? "No--" He swallowed hard. "No survivors."

"Get our friend to quarantine." Captain Tyrell said. "I want to know why they want him, and what they don't want us to know."

"Three more ships coming from the direction of the planet, their weapons are charged." There was a tone. "This is patrol ship Firefox, you destroyed our ship you will be destroyed."

"Channel is closed. Firing."

"Absorption shields to max," the captain said. "All hands, brace."

The ship shimmied this time under the combined and sustained blast, but other than a few stations sparking and a jolt that might have knocked some people off their feet, there was no problem.

"Minimal damage, mostly internal systems." Jenna said.

Tyrell nodded. Now he was angry. "Squadron seven, join your compatriots please, delta defense."

He took two deep breaths to consider his actions trying to avoid bowing to the anger that Girati were so well known for. "All CQWS, target propulsion and weapons. Leave them dead in the water and defenseless, but take your shots carefully. Remember, these ships don't have our shielding."

"They are trying to call a rally point; they are calling for a heavy destroyer." Comms said. "Jammed the whole band, but we can't hold it long."

"That's our cue. Take out the comms system and sensors and set a course for that planet. If they don't want us there, we better see just what they don't want us to see."

"Aye sir, spikes away, ships are disabled." The weapons officer said.

As they set course for the planet, the captain wished AJ was here in the pilot's seat. That would calm his nerves.

On the flight deck, the lights dimmed, allowing the pilots heads up systems to work. And the comms chirped for them. "Rails One and seven are live, one and seven are live," came the modulated voice of the computer. Within moments of the change in the light level, there was noise and movement as pilots began jumping from their bunks and finishing dressing in the low light. As they finished, they gathered toward the center. The eight rails branched off in Vs from where they were and they gathered.

"Single squad so far, the rest are on standby. Only half the rails are working, so be aware of your launch number." The squadron commander said, as he read over the incident report feeding to the main system. "You should have plenty of room so don't pull up, just ride the wake all the way out. And remember, your rails have a lot of punch but you can't fire them like a laser, you gotta wait for them to reset, and you gotta be ready for the recoil."

This system was still new. This was their first live engagement. "Remember, once your rail is locked you gotta hold steady, and for gods sake make sure you're clear before you fire, I don't want you spiking your own boys." There was nervous laughter because in the sims some of them had been spiked. But this was their first actual engagement with the enemy.

"Now commander Henson will say a few words."

"You soft-skins are far too unskilled for this, and far too untrained, but I don't have anyone better."

Tucura didn't believe in compliments. By now, the crew was used to the reverse pep talks. They'd been training with the Tucura for a year before the fighters went live, and at the station they had run drills every day to get up to speed on the rails.

"Flight Captain Jonas has the rail." The Tucuran said as he slunk away. The Tucuran commanders hated being here, but those were the orders from command and a Tucuran didn't disobey unless they were prepared to kill or die.

Jonas stood and pulled on his helmet. "All right vipers, as far as we know these are the guys who got Jeffries, so we are going to go out there and show them why they don't mess with us, and why they don't mess with the captain. There is a civilian out there in the debris, we need to bring him back alive."

"Watch your launchers. Leave 27 on the rack, we're flying missing man." Jonas said. They all touched launch tube 27 as they went to their spots.

The squadron commander, a Tucurn, frowned, of course, they always frowned, they lacked the cleft under their noses to be able to smile. SUDEC, Small, Ultra-sonic Defense and Exploration Craft were rail-launched fighters. This particular set was the two-seat Defense craft, everything that wasn't shields or weapons had been stripped, and they could be launched from still to half light in under five seconds. Now, being that this was a close launch, they were not being launched as fast.

"Rails' are hot, targeting up, friend-foe active, and CQWS have our scans." Squad leader said.

The Close Quarters Weapons System had to have a scan of the ships so it wouldn't accidentally track them. CQWS were small rail guns that could hurl solid projectiles, depleted nuclear or solid ion rounds right now. They were using standard solid explosive projectiles, called Spikes. Spikes were about six feet long and a foot in diameter, and when they hit something at near-light, just the wake could cause difficulties. They could be hurled with surprising accuracy over long distances, and were able to penetrate most shields and hull plates in a single blow. Which is why, much to the annoyance of the Tucura, they often aimed for non-Personnel areas.

"CQWS are online." The ship shook as the weapons spun up and fired.

They were all heading for their canopies. Jeffries wasn't flying today, and was actually kind of glad. He was playing mission command from the bridge, where he had a perfect view of the battle.

"Hold!" he said as the ship came into view. "Lock launchers,' BRACE!"

Statues

At the time he said it, going down seemed like the best idea in the world. The paint wasn't even dry yet, and Captain Tyrell was on an away mission to save... Well, he didn't know who they were there to rescue, just that there was more of the crystal, and somewhere in there was a life sign.

There was something about the place where they landed. Once they came over the ridge, their sensors gave only nonsense. Shapes and half-shapes, and lives that weren't alive, and bodies that weren't dead, everything seemed to be in a state of flux. Over everything was a purple hue. That alone set his teeth on edge. Why, he couldn't say. But as they came over the ridge into what looked like a crater, that warning of the Girati went off. Something was seriously wrong. What they found was what was left of a ship, her hull long since lost to age, leaving spires attached to nothing, and gaping holes. Nearby on the plain were statues, hundreds of them. There were no plaques, no names, nothing to tell who they were, they simply were. Some standing, some kneeling, a few laying with red crystal around them.

Whatever this place was, it was evil, and it turned his senses just to be here. It was more of the purple crystal that had taken one of his crew. He approached slowly, walking between the statues, careful not to touch them. As he moved, it seemed that some of them did too. Arms would be different, legs would be different, all of them slowly moving in one direction around a central spire, an obelisk.

Lightning cracked, lighting up the area, but Tyrell wasn't paying attention. He was looking at the statues, and he crept closer to the central spire. As much as he was afraid, he wasn't terrified, nowhere near as afraid as he needed to be. It was a single ring of a dozen statues, standing, back to the obelisk, arms above their heads, wrists crossed, the age-old Girati pose of Danger that told him what this was, why this was, and how much danger he was in. Purple. A stone walked.

Another crack of lightning lit up the area, showing in the purple crystal the figure with the high hair, the Mistress. Tyrell stopped suddenly as if he himself had been turned to stone. His heart hammering in his ears as his brain churned through what he knew. He reached down, taking a handful of sand from the ground he tossed it in the air and spoke a prayer.

"GO!" he charged back toward the ridgeline. "No names, no words, Just run, run or it will take us too."

Few of these men had ever heard of this man afraid, and this—this was beyond afraid. For the first time in his long life, Tyrell was terrified, heart-wrenching, night-sweats when remembered years later; that sort of terrified. What was here was something they didn't understand, something they were not equipped to deal with, and something that would eat them alive. When they made it back to the shuttle, he still refused to speak, refused to tell them what he saw. He just shook his head. And his body, long used to following his command, didn't now, and shook. Whatever he had seen had scared him more than anything else ever could.

The Living Stone

Tyrell's first thought when he saw their refugee was that someone had given him payback. But then he saw that many of the bruises were colored and the nosebleed was from a Reprimand. If this young man hadn't been a Unit, he would have been dead. And that was probably the reason he had called for asylum.

He recognized him instantly. It was the young man who had shown him to his quarters. But somewhere deep inside, there was a deeper recognition. He knew this boy, but he didn't know where from. It was the same recognition as the dream. But he didn't notice that.

"Wo-would it be ok sir if I pulled up my sleeves?"

"Of course."

The young man did nothing.

Tyrell sighed. "Yes, it is ok."

"Thank you, sir." He rolled up his sleeves and, on his right arm was a small scar, one Tyrell recognized. It was a blooding mark, part of a Girati's coming of age. Depending on the ship and situation they could be as young as twelve and they could be as old as fifty. Though a Girati of fifty wouldn't look his age. But it did explain why his face was familiar. Though on closer inspection, it wasn't real, it couldn't be real, there was something... not right about it, like the one that the pilot had worn it was fake, and though a better fake, made by one who had seen them, it was a fake that only fooled him for a moment.

Still he took the hint that the young man was Girati. Though that confused him, many of his manners were also Clatch, the Terran natives that dressed in grey, and there was no way he was both, not unless he was much, much older than he let on... But even then... why had no one come looking for him? The kin didn't care if you were a Unit. You were kin. Maybe it was an affect? Some sort of attempt to blend in?

"Your song betrays your blood," he said, a traditional way of telling a Girati that you are one too. He was trying to understand who and what this young man was. Though he was beginning to feel that he might not be as young as he claimed.

"Y—I'm sorry I don't understand what you are talking about."

The quick change was no doubt spurred on by a Reprimand.

Or was it? There was something fighting against the computer. Something, Tyrell hated to say it, something more powerful. He barely dared to think the thought that settled in his mind. "Its the living stone."

Tyrell decided to see how deep this rabbit hole went and if this young man even knew he was being used as a pawn. He started with standard questions.

"So, K101, why are they willing to kill themselves than to let you go?" he sild closer.

"There is a field of the nameless, and there is her, the nameless, but we knew her long ago, you and I, we knew her name, but it is taken from me and forgotten by you." The voice sounded afraid and certainly younger than his face, but not quite childish. Stuck somewhere between Unit and Child, the voice was unusual.

The young man's eyes were glassy, and it was clear that he was in some sort of altered state. Tyrell touched the young man in an attempt to wake him, and for a moment K-101 seemed lucid. His words, though, were still rambling and without any focus.

"They have names, the nameless, I was supposed to be one, but I would not give up my name, I would not be what they wanted me to be, and so they took my name."

"Who are they?" Tyrell asked.

"The men of blood with daggers on their sleeves. I went for help and instead they brought me back to him, I tried to warn them that they didn't know, didn't understand but there were no words, he stopped me, and they took my name so I could not stop him. They took everything. They took the only hope of stopping him, of making her whole, but they didn't know, wanted a weapon, wouldn't listen when we told them it wouldn't work as they wanted.

"K101, what was your name?" He had to help the boy remember his name. If he could remember that, maybe he could wrest control from the stone.

"Name? There is no name, only the purple mist, the song, and the statues. There is something there, someone but I don't know her, I can't know her. I know her, but the memory is taken."

The Purity patrol had tried to wipe his memory, but fragments of the memory remained. And he was stuck trying to string them into a coherent order, and leaving him open for the living stone to take total control.

"You mentioned a sister, "Tyrell asked. "Where is she?"

"She is gone, away, and away, he took her away and away with the song." The stone-boy replied.

"Your sister, is she dead?" Tyrell was trying to figure out the references.

"Not dead, gone." He smiled. "But not gone. Here, but not."

Nothing else the boy said seemed at all lucid.

"Keep recording, see if he says anything else interesting. I'm going to be in my ready room trying to make sense of all of this."

The surrounding image was one she knew, one she trusted. It was the cold grid. Pulsing lines of power, buildings and parks built into the computer-scape. Cold grid was fusion of computer and time grid. Part of the damage from the accident that destroyed most of the time hubs.

It created the creatures that were called Wraith by humans because they never saw the sun so they were pale, and their eyes, once converted, were red, and held no shine of life because they were computer.

Standing on the grid was the young man who was now in holding.

"You know what I am." The young man asked.

"Go away, Murderer!" Jenna found herself speaking before she could stop herself.

"You hate me for a crime that is not mine." The stone-boy replied.

"You are a Unit." She repeated.

"Before that I was a man." He reminded Jenna.

"So?" Jenna asked. She tilted her head to look at him.

"I was changed against my will, as we all were. And you know what it is to live and die by ones and zeroes, but that is not what I came to talk about. I know you have seen her, the little girl." The eyes of the young man glowed purple, and his whole manner of standing changed, but the computer wasn't powered. She would know if it was. "You have seen her. She is a danger, she will steal this ship, she will destroy it, just like the others, she is a threat. "You must kill her. Before she does to your ship what she did to the Black Star."

Jenna was tempted, but something was wrong. "Your computer is dormant, so who is speaking? These are not human words, humans would care for their sisters, so who is this?"

"This is the one without a name." He smiled. "You are smarter than I thought. Far too smart for such a doomed ship."

"How is it doomed?"

"It will die, it will blow up just as the Dark Star did." The voice was a little different now as the stone stopped hiding its presence.

"You set the bomb?"

"No, but your captain will, he will light this ship to keep me off, he will kill his family to save them, just as he did before. Except that time he ran away, he didn't stay to help. He didn't mourn them, just forgot them and ran away, and he will forget you too, just a fragment of a program."

Jenna knew this was what passed for a dream for her, but she didn't dream like humans. It was always here, and they were almost always bad dreams. A rain of code began and she rewrote the dream just like she was reprogramming a computer and in a moment was the waterfall at the end of the grid. All was silence, but she couldn't quite shake the idea, the feeling of danger.

Fallen

THE CAPTAIN WAS TRYING to reconcile what he knew with what he'd been told. He wanted to believe K101, but the young man hadn't been lucid in generations, probably. His body was older, but something powerful had stunted his mind. He could pretend, but sometimes, many times now, he couldn't, and the original age came through. The captain's mind rebelled at the truth. But this was what happened when a living stone took over a human form.

He paced, coffee in hand, listening to the recording of K-101 looking for a way to stop this stone. "We were there, on steel, but not our steel. And it was cold, alone, silent." The voice sounded childish, even on the record. "And the song was there but it was distant, and everything was cold, and then it was away and away and away, and there were people, and the song again, but then it was hot, bright, song, and then cold, alone, silent, and away and away and away."

"That happened many times." The voice sounded afraid. The man wasn't being questioned. He had just started babbling as soon as he had been rescued. They had tried to ask him what was going on, but his lucidity only lasted a few minutes. "He said it was because they wanted to hurt us, and that we were friends, but we didn't like the alone. We should have told father that we took him in, but father wouldn't stop to listen.

"The voices were loud, and the crystal shard we found was so bright. So pretty, so we took it, and we played with it. And one day it spoke to us. And he said his name was Borei, and that he was happy to have friends, and he would protect us forever.

"And he would hum this melody, and the world seemed-- better for a while, and then anger, and when the anger came, so would the purple light, and then the silence. And away and away."

"Pause recording."

The story was told with the halting words of a child. "Away and away" was a Girati construction used by younger children for a long distance or a long time. And for the children in the rift to find a crystal, possibly from one of their own versions... that must have been strange. They wouldn't have known it was dangerous.

A single shard of a broken stone was enough to infect if the stone walked. He wished he could ask if Borei's stone was purple, but a sliver of a house-stone. The large control stones that bound them together as a crew, would be more than enough to overwhelm a pair of children. Which he and his sister must have been.

"Resume."

"It sang a sad song at first, telling us that its steel was gone. That's what it called the ship. 'Steel" Stej, it said, "The Steel' and it called itself "Sten'a" or "The stone.' And it said that its job was to sing so the ship could go faster. I wanted to tell Papa, but the stone, Borei, didn't want us to."

"Pause recording. Computer, lookup Borei, all variants, limit search to Terran usage please."

"Working...." There was silence a moment. "Borei, Terran, Japanese, "bent or twisted soul" used for demons and ghosts in Japanese Mythology pre-war."

"Is there any correlation between PC and Japan?"

"Nine of the First Fleet Ships came from the Commonwealth of Japan. Their flagship was—" The screen printed the letters as the ship's computer tried to pronounce the language no one had heard in centuries. "Songubādo"

"Would that be Songbird in Terran Standard?"

"Affirmative."

"Continue playback."

"We could hear the song, the music and it was beautiful, but far too loud. He said it was loud because there were none, no protectors, no Father, no Mistress of the stone... He said that was how it was, that she was the mistress of the stone, and he was the Father of the Steel, she helped him sing, and he kept her safe so she could sing... but it was all silent and away and away, many times away, out to the black and back, and back and back. But always children. They hid us away, never old enough to come of age, never old enough because of our friend, but we eventually learned he wasn't a friend. When Papa became the first statue."

"Stop playback." The first statue. the purple statues he had seen down there, living stone subsumed them utterly. He took a long sip of coffee. The hot drink settled his nerves, it was something normal, something that couldn't hurt him.

The timeline was jumbled, as any child's story was, but he started to be able to make sense of it. But whatever else, he had to hear it from the boy. "A whispered song, a melody to share, listen to me, and I will ease your care." The sound wasn't loud enough to really be heard or understood, it was a telepathic phrase, and the stone had worked hard on it. But, he had found out it only works on Girati. It made them easy to confuse, and easy to compel.

"Come to me, listen to me, give me what I need," the stone whispered. It had invaded the small shards that were worn by both the boy and girl. But fortunately, it had not taken over the Captain's shard, not yet. The overwhelming grief prevented it.

"Captain, please, give me what you do not claim to have, that thing you would never admit, she must die!" The young man was agitated, and had been for the past thirty minutes. "You have met her, she will not stop until this ship is nameless."

"It already is," he said to the young man. "And I have heard the story of the stone."

K101 laughed. "Then you are the only one who can do it. Without a name there is no control, and he cannot take what is not his. He took ours and made it quiet. We were saved, he said, because we were innocent, we had done no wrong, but we were too young to do anything wrong... Too young..."

Tyrell was too lost in thought, too lost in could be's and maybes and might be's to pay attention to what the boy was saying, especially when it didn't sound lucid.

"Please captain, give me that which none will admit to carrying, give me what I ask and let me kill her." He twitched. "Please, please, you must, she has killed too many, she has killed many many ships, there is nothing to do but kill her before she gets your ship too. Before she destroys us all."

Tyrell didn't ask the question he should have asked. He didn't ask about who she was before. He didn't ask about what happened before they were taken by the stone. His mind was consumed with the thoughts of others losing their ships as he had lost his, and that pain and anguish. For others, like the Black Star, it had to be done.

He heard the same melody that he had heard in his ready room, a psychic ear-worm, a repeated thought that moved him on reflex without aid of his higher brain function. It made his logical brain sleepy and sedate, and made him act on instinct.

His hands had moved nearly of their own accord when he was brought out of it by a chime. His first officer and assembled staff were waiting. He'd have to talk to them before he did anything. That was his duty as the captain, and he'd have to carry that weight.

The effect of the music was less, now that he was concentrating on something. And the song dimmed to less than a breath, just enough to keep control, but not enough to move him.

And it was difficult to dislodge. To do so, you had to get him thinking, questioning, asking more than yes-no-maybe questions. Tyrell didn't understand that he was being controlled by a subtle kind of mind control. It was one so insidious that even the Girati who normally fight against it wouldn't notice it. It was the type of mind control that made one remember the ills without remembering the good. So one would remember the pain of loss, but not the happiness of memory, and one would never think of what the others would want.

As The captain stepped out of the brig cell, Toru came to him, putting a hand on his shoulder and bringing him back to himself fully. Dark eyes looked at the captain and the close-cropped head shook sadly. "It is as I feared." He patted him on the back and turned him to leave the brig. "The others are assembled; we've been trying to reach you."

"Oh, yes. I'm sorry, I must have lost track of time." He looked at the chrononometer to find he had been staring at the wall for almost an hour.

The responses were still stilted and not quite on target, so he stopped in the hall. "Captain Hansen, pull yourself together." Toru frowned. "Whatever has your mind is taking you on dangerous circles."

To be spoken to like that by a Shedda was quite a dressing down. The captain frowned and took a deep breath. He felt like Toru had just doused him in cold water. "Thank you, friend, I think my head is clear now." He gestured for him to continue to walk. "Shall we? I believe the crew awaits."

It was a fiction; it was a play-act that he was well. He smiled and breathed properly, but still the melody in the back of his mind was making his conscious brain sleepy, allowing him to act on emotion and instinct. Toru kept his counsel for a moment. He figured having more than himself might finally shake whatever had the captain's mind so badly altered. If the captain had been anyone else, he would have been tempted to take command, but he knew Tyrell. He knew his reputation for being rock solid. So whatever this was would affect whoever was in command. He was better off being here, at his side, to try to work on the psychic bond coming from the world below.

There was no doubt in his mind that this had infiltrated his dreams, but he concluded it was not connected to the bomb. The bomb was purely human. This was something more, something frightening.

The Story of the First

"If I may be so bold, Captain?"

"You may," Tyrell said, as he respected Toru's input.

And after their talk in the hall, he wanted to know what he had nearly done to get the Shedda equivalent to a tongue-lashing. For a Shedda to tell you you are entering dangerous circles was for them to say whatever you were about to do, wasn't just dangerous, but capable of destroying the life you know.

Whatever strange control the prisoner had over him extended even this far away. No one saw where he had pulled it from but in his hands was the tiny purple vial of poison. "That which we would never admit to carrying.", as they said. Suicide and murder was not common among the Girati except the odd crime of passion. This poison was made for one purpose and one purpose only, to defend against a walking stone. To kill you and destroy your cells enough that the stone could not use you as a host.

As a Shedda, Toru knew of poisons and that one was one of the deadliest and most horrific ever invented. There was no immunity, it either killed you or it ravaged you so completely that you were never quite the same, and to let that fall into the hands of another, and worse yet, to let it be used to kill another Girati, no matter the reason, was a crime for which there was no forgiveness.

"Your grief and anger is leading you to a rather—human solution." He said simply. "We know what the captain would do, but the question you need to ask, before you give him that—"

He nodded at the vial so deadly even the Girati wouldn't speak of it. "Is that what would the Fe'an do?" He knew the words were different even though they would be translated the same. The "fe'an" translated better as "Father," or father-protector. It was his job to care for his family. It was for him to help those on his steel and keep them from making rash decisions. Girati were known for their temper, both in anger, and in learning to control or temper it. In this case, he was fueled by one and forgetting the other.

Toru gestured to the rest of those assembled, security, navigation, defense craft, medical, engineering, they were all represented. "Your men will fight 'to the man' for you, but they may not have to." The Girati phrase meant to fight to the death. Or 'to the last man' from whence came the Girati phrase.

"Look past the pain of loving and losing, and think like this is your steel, what would the Fe'an do? There may not be a stone, but she has her own song. So listen and stop being—human."

The humans in the room grimaced but understood. There were some things that humans did well and death was one of them.

The last vestige of the control slipped, and Tyrell looked at what he had clutched in his hand, his heart hammering as he looked at the deadly purple vial that was not much bigger than an old Terran kitchen match.

"What would the Fe'an do?" he asked aloud.

After a moment of thought he answered his own question. "Find out what she wants." He looked at the poison, death was a human answer. She might die, but it would not be by his hand.

Not willingly. This, Toru was right, would have been murder. The vial vanished as quickly as it appeared, and no one saw where it went.

He turned back to the assembled leaders of their departments. Jenna, Toru, one of the ensigns from engineering, while Sampson fixed the engine, the doctor, the pilot Jeffries, standing in for Abby—for Abby, in her honor this had to be solved, and it had to be better than cheapening her death by giving into his fear as the other captain had.

"Though I fear, my fear does not control me, I find my notes in the song and I know my place," he said softly to himself. And the fear began to recede. He took a deep breath. Now re-centered he made a motion asking pardon. And received a wave in response, as if 'its nothing' was the reply.

This then, was what had caused the captain of the other ship to destroy it. If the stone could not have the ship, it would destroy it.

"What do we know about her, the girl from the dream? What does she want?" he asked, his voice now stronger than it had been. "She's a child. And the debris have this mark on them."

Jeffries, the real one was sitting there for Abby. He reached over and thumbed the control that lit up the screen. The name was all but illegible but a small bird was still visible. "We checked the records and this emblem is old, really old, in fact, it's forbidden for any modern ship to carry this emblem. It is from First Fleet. The Psychic Conglomerate ship, Songbird."

"PC Songbird..." he continued. "It was one of the original hundred ships to which the Girati trace their lineage, but sometime, between three and five thousand years ago, it is said that she floated into the rift. And, of course, we know that time in and around the rift does funny things, so that three hundred Terran years can become nearly nine thousand at the rift. And if conjecture is right, she drifted out following the N-space corridor here and crashed on the planetoid."

"Thank you, Jeffries." He smiled. "So we know this is a ship we haven't seen in forever, a ship that is pre-stone. So what we have to ask, is what does she want?" There was something he still wasn't seeing. Some part that was still lost to him, being so modern.

"Well—" The doctor stood there, looking at Jenna and then Jeffries. "If your dreams are anything like mine, she seemed familiar, and asked me if I knew her name."

"Name..." The captain said. "Doc, what would you put her age at?" It hit him suddenly. The piece that had been missing. She kept asking for a name, her name. Why didn't she know her own name, and why could none of them remember it?

"Eight, ten, maybe?" He frowned. "I don't understand, what does age have to do with it?"

"Too young for an Aja." The captain said. "I think I know why she seems so familiar to us, and only us."

"What?" The doctor asked as he flipped through the medical logs. He understood what the captain was getting at, that no one but them had had the dreams, not a single person on the ship besides probably AJ.

"Doctor, have any of the crew besides us, come in with the nightmare we've had, about the girl?"

"No, just us, and Sampson." He had checked twice.

"That's what I thought. We all have learned about the Girati. Funny things, dreams, you hear in a language you may not speak anymore, but you understand, and sometimes you forget to pay attention. When she said YOU, it was the Formal group you. "You all" or "All Girati" because she doesn't have a name, she has many." The captain smiled because it finally clicked how he knew her. "Any of you hear the tale of the Songbird?"

"The first ship, they all went crazy right?" That was the doctor. "We studied it in Interspecies medicine and psychic phenomenon."

"That's the legend. It was a cautionary tale, but every ship told it with different names. Songbird, with that emblem had been missing for generations, it was first fleet. Before we had stones."

"What?" That didn't compute to Jenna.

We didn't have stones, not the ones that ran the ship, and not the shards we carried that bound us to the steel." Tyrell said. "Imagine, all the power of the Girati, and no stone to temper it." But the story has a part most people forget. If a stone walks, it needs a human host, but if the human can name himself, he or she can take control and force the stone to leave."

"She's been asking for help for centuries, but no one stopped to listen to her. No one bothered to answer her question, or to ask why she didn't know her name. They just reacted to the threat, and the stone destroyed them as an open threat."

"So she needs this—stone?" Jenna asked.

"No, in this case, the stone is the problem. She's pre-stone. I don't know where it came from, but she didn't know how to use it, and doesn't have a link to it to control it, nor is there enough crew to mute it." He frowned. "K-101 was rambling in the brig, but in amongst the rambling is a story. A very familiar story. She and her brother were playing, probably with stuff they found in cargo bay, castoffs, broken stuff, and among what they had dredged to sell when they could was a fragment of stone. And the stone became her friend. But he's far too powerful without a ship, without a crew, and without the Chezan to temper it. But binding her to the stone would just give it control."

"Couldn't you make her free singer?" Jeffries asked.

The room went silent for a moment. "Explain," Tyrell said. No one but the captain understood that term as he meant it.

"If she's needing a name, she needs a steel too, right? So make her family, give her a name and a ship. Her ship. Hers to protect and control. That's what the Mistress does right? And the Fe'an protects her so that she doesn't have to. But neither of them know what they are supposed to do," He said, "To put it in perspective, it's like they've forgotten the rest of the story. So if we tell them who they are, we can tell them the story of how to free themselves."

"But how do we give them a name?" Jenna asked, she was the least familiar with the Girati.

"Same way I was given a new name." Jeffries said. "Ajari can be used to make a ship Girati right? But you can take a new name, I did. Jeffries is my given name, but I have a Girati name that only AJ knows, and maybe the captain. So, we give her a new name, and a new ship—well, an old ship, but we make it hers. And we give her the power to stop the stone, and if she can't then we fall back on the other plan. But we should answer her question first."

"I agree, and I'm going to need all of you. Jenna, you are going to have to stay here and work from here on fixing the damage and making sure those bastards didn't get a readable signal through. Scramble where we are, and start on quarantine pods, I want to put this whole planetoid under permanent quarantine." He frowned. "It's too dangerous to take you down there. Your bio implants might be just the thing the stone needs, and I don't want to get that sort of tech anywhere near that stone.

"Engineering, Work on repairing any damage both by the explosive being there and the programs that got hacked, when I come back I expect to be able to go out to the rim and back on these engines. And keep some in reserve in case we need to get out of here in a hurry. I don't look for trouble, but it may follow. We don't know if there are other ships on the way."

"Aye sir." The young ensign ran off to tell the Chief engineer.

"Toru, normally, I would give you the bridge, but I need you down there to keep my head clear. You seem to be able to deal with whatever they are broadcasting better than I am, and I can't afford a slip like earlier."

"Of course, Captain." He bowed. Psychic assaults like this were simple for him to defeat, it was his stock-in-trade.

He placed a hand on the captain's shoulder. "I have faith in you, Captain. Do not let your worry for AJ and your sorrow for Abby cloud your mind. There are many more lives at stake."

"Thank you."

The second landing crew was the captain, Jeffries, the doctor, K101, and Toru.

"While we are here touch nothing. Speak nothing and stick to your script. Toru put a hand on the captain's back, a silent show of support before they all moved out. And with that single touch, Toru gave the captain a mental push past the melody that had caught him earlier.

As they came over the rise, all of them tried not to look at the statues.

"Alira?" The captain called. He knocked on the bulkhead. "We are friends of the Song, Visitors from far away, we ask leave to enter, we mean no harm to any on this steel who be men and women of good faith."

It was the normal leave to enter, for a moment he had thought to use the quarantine one, but he was afraid that might set the stone off, so right now, it was just business as usual and Toru running interference not only with the psychic wave that had caught him, but also to blunt their thoughts so the stone couldn't read them.

There was lightning and then the girl was there, her eyes glowing purple. "You are heard. You may enter."

"For the dishonor last time." The captain pricked his finger. "I pay the debt that we owe, for we did not know this was your steel."

"It is forgiven, and paid." The girl smiled. "What was that name?"

"Alira? That is your name."

"My name? I don't remember my name."

"No, you don't." The captain knelt to her level. He checked her arm. Her skin was ice cold. She was not much more than a puppet, a doll, but he had to hope since she wasn't yet stone, that some of her mind still existed. "You have no Ajari, let me give you back your name."

"You would do that?"

"Of course, I would, we only forgot because it was so long ago. It's been centuries and centuries, before stones and songs, you were away long, long ago." He smiled. "You were away and away and away the song is much softer now, not as deafening, so sometimes it hard to hear.

She nodded. "What about my brother?" She nodded to K-101

"We brought him back to you." Tyrell said. "He was the one who told us the story. We are sorry it took so long. But we know his name too. He is Chezir."

"What do they mean?" she asked. Her voice fading from the many-voice of the stone to the child.

"Your name is 'Song of the Universe' or 'Song of the People.' Your brother is 'Protector of the Song.'"

They both smiled. The fake mark disappeared from K101's arm. It was like everything else, a memory of what it should be. Everything here was a memory of a story. The dreams, the rambling, it was all the story of the songbird, but told in so many different voices, by so many different crews, it was impossible to keep straight. Raw power of the stone, it corrupted, not morally, but it twisted everything it touched. The only way the Girati were able to control it was by sharing it. Sharing it with blood family. Thus the Aja. "We are happy, but he is not."

"He can't touch us. Right now, you have given us permission to be here, and we have done no harm."

"So what do we do?" She asked. Her eyes were brown now. Not bright purple, as her own mind took over from the stone.

Seeing the change, the Captain reached out his hands to both children. "Give me your arms, quickly."

The captain knew they didn't have time to waste, it would only be a matter of time before the stone realized it was losing its hold, he just had to get this done before the stone figured it out, and the best way to do that was concentrate on projecting normalcy and calm.

Both K101 and the girl presented their right arms to him. "K101 is not a name, it is a designation, and today I take it from you, and break its power," he said, pulling the name patch off the uniform. "With these as our witnesses, we will give you your names, and your Steel."

The captain spoke a few words in Girati and cut the small mark on their arms, turning them so they bled onto the steel.

Then he rubbed the blood into the steel with his boot. "Your blood is on the steel, the steel is in your blood; this ship, the Songbird, is yours to protect and yours to live in."

"Mine?" The brown eyes looked up and the ship creaked as she tried to build it beyond the three foot level.

"Yes, Mistress." He placed his hands, thumb and forefinger together to form a diamond shape against his forehead, then he bowed, the sign for a Reverence. "You are Mistress of this steel, and the stone, the stone is not bound to this ship, this ship is, and always has been free steel."

"Free steel?" She was curious. "You mean without stone or song?" Neither she nor hier brother moved.

Tyrell nodded, seeing the purple cast coming again he explained quickly. "They may have them, and use them, but they do not need them. I do not know where this stone came from, but he is not of the steel. You have your name, use it. The story that always changes, that is never the same, and that always ends in sadness, its over. You have your names, your true names."

Her eyes went purple as the stone tried to take over. For a moment, nothing happened, but then K101, Chezir as they now called him, "the protector of the song," spoke. "Stone, I name you, Interloper." Chezir said, pointing to his sister and then to the obelisk. "This is not your steel. You hold no blood here, and our song and your song are different. My name is Protector of the all-song, and you are not wanted here."

Her eyes returned to the right color. And then she spoke. "Stone of ages, I name you." Alira said, "Murderer, Kin-killer, silencer of the song." The captain winced. Those were the worst insults among the Girati.

"This is my steel, And these are my crew, And I want you out." For a moment it seemed that her hair, down, and long was blown up into the fan of Mistress. "Be gone!"

Far in the distance the obelisk cracked. "And I decree from this moment on, stone without blood may not pass this steel. And there are none left for you to take. You will not murder anymore."

This time her eyes glowed white, as any Mistress' might when she was angry. And, in the distance the statues began to move. Gesturing to the captain and his small party, she spoke. "These are my Chosen, leave them be," she said to the statues.

"Tear down the stone, break it, destroy it, drown out it's song we are the all-song. We are the crew of the Songbird, and we will not be forgotten again!"

The song that had been plaguing the captain was suddenly gone. In its place was a melody of a united ship, angry and alive, it reverberated with the rage of an enslaved crew. The eyes of the statues began to glow, not purple, but white. And the statues went from purple to red, and then to yellow, the sign of stone that has not been bound. Slowly the stone statues turned red again, this time the deep crimson of the Girati Crystal and the statues began to move. Now they turned toward the obelisk and they began to move like a wave of glass. Only the twelve protectors did not change. So totally taken by the stone they could not turn, their crystal became purple but laced with black. Sick and broken.

Their eyes glowed dimly purple, but they could not fight the bright white of the crew.

To the Girati in the team the cacophony was deafening for a moment, and then it was muted, and a harmony. Angry, and tired, but harmony. "When the stone has gone, we commend you to your rest, do not plague the living. And we will be sure that few if any ever come here again to wake you."

The statues closed in on the living stone, now that they faced away from the crew, the white light was lessened, and aimed at the obelisk. There was a melody, it was nearly palpable, and it sang of justice, not revenge. But for a moment, one statue turned and smiled at them. "Tana Ke Gira," it mouthed, its voice long since lost. And then it turned back to the obelisk and joined the fight. The outline of a flight suit could just be seen under the crystal.

"Go," Alira said. She looked spent, and much older than her child form, a grandmother of grandmothers she seemed now.

"Go with my blessing, I cannot keep control much longer. I am dying and he will seek new blood if I am dead. Leave us to our song, and eternal rest." She spoke to the statues. "A little louder, children, sing together of the crimes he has committed, and force him back, break him, smash him, grind him to dust that no man may ever hear his song again."

"Go Fe'an Tyrell, go in peace and may their memories bring you only peace and happiness."

"Thank you for your hospitality. We leave you to your rest and will sing the songs of lament for you. We will carry your names in our hearts. The captain bent down and pulled a loose shard of hull plate. "If I may, I will take this, to show others that this was no dream."

"Take it." She smiled. "Thank you, Captain. You were the first to ever answer my question. Most tried to kill me."

"Here is my failure, I would have too, had not these brought me back to myself."

She smiled. "Is that not what family and crew is for?"

The captain had backed away, still not turning in case she wished to speak again. "Your brother's song is strong, he will live," she said as the captain turned his back and walked away.

He wasn't sure if he had heard it or not, but he dared not call back over his shoulder.

"Today, no longer shall you be called Nameless, but Alira, the singer of the Songbird, savior of the First world."

Aftermath

The captain sat in his ready room, trying to figure out how to write up the incident that had just happened. The door beeped and when he asked for them to enter, it turned out to be Jenna.

"The warns have been set. And there is also a dampening field that should stop any propulsion system. The penalty for going to that planet is death, and it is death to take any crystal from it." She bared her teeth, a sign she was not happy. "I know this is harsh for your liking, but it really is the only option." They'd had this talk twice already. Girati were not usually ones to impose a death penalty, but if even one shard was still alive and left the planet, there might be trouble.

"I know. Girati are not cowards, we will kill, it's just not our first option."

"I know, Captain. And it is something I am learning to not be my first option." Jenna said. Her awkward smile was very violent, but she was trying.

"Good. Then we have both learned something." He thought a moment. "I need you to write up what we know about the crystal, get with the Doctor about it. Now that we know what it's capable of, I want options in case we meet anymore. Hopefully all of it died when the stone shattered, but maybe not. So,

I want you and the doctor to find a way to combat it, hopefully without losing the host, but if that is the only way, at least to keep it from spreading."

"Yes, sir," She said. "Anything else?"

"No, that's it."

She started to walk away. "I know it may not be my place, Captain, and we all grieve in our own way, but maybe you should read that notice."

"What does it say?" the captain asked.

"The crew has put together a memorial for K101, Abby, and the crew of the songbird, they would be honored if you would attend."

"Thank you."

"One more thing, Captain." She turned back.

"Yes?"

"I know that your grief has blinded you, but you must learn when to listen to your Girati instinct, and when to listen to human emotion. Like me, Captain, you are half human, all Girati are. Most of their DNA is the same as the humans. All that to say, I understand what it means to not feel like you don't belong anywhere. But a wise man once told me that he believed in me, Wraith or no, so I have to to tell that wise man, that I believe in him, human or Girati, just don't become so USL you forget to be Girati."

"Thank you, Jenna."

"What is family for?" She smiled the odd-toothy grin again, for the first time in a long time she felt like maybe she did have a place.

That's what Alira had asked. If not to shake you out of your stupor of grief, what else is family for? A shared grief is less deep. And the pain of losing crew so soon, it still hurt. And in some ways, he blamed himself, even though he knew there was nothing he could have done.

"That song is sung, there is no re-singing," he told himself. "You can't change the notes now, and it does no good to wonder what would have been," he reminded himself.

Finally, he opened the letter he'd been avoiding, the one inviting him to the memorial. But he was surprised to find that it was a Girati remembrance of lights. He smiled. In so many ways they were mindful of his past. As if they had been crew for ages not a week.

There might still be arguments and misunderstandings, but for the most part the crew respected him, and his command crew, they, all in their own way, loved him. He was the Fe'an of the ship, the father, the protector, it was his job to make the hard choices so others didn't have to. But it was also his job to show them that he could mourn the necessity of those choices too.

"Computer, suspend this terminal."

"Affirmative."

A thumb swipe locked it, and he walked out of the ready room feeling better than he had in a long time.

The captain was surprised when he came to the landing bay to find lanterns, hundreds of them. At one end of the bay stood Jeffries. He knew it was going to be a remembrance of the lights, but he had forgotten how many crew a Girati ship could have. "1393, the number of crew of the Songbird, including the Fe'an and the Mistress, and the crew that we lost, Abby. There are no bodies to bury, or to send out into space, as they normally do, so

I checked their history, and a festival of lights, such as this, was an acceptable substitute." He handed the captain a lighter.

"And we have some nameless for the victims of the stone we may not yet know. And we hope that is acceptable."

The captain nodded. "its perfect." He gestured for silence and stillness.

"Not all of you understand the significance of these lights. When Girati die, their bodies are given to the universe. They are allowed to drift until a black hole or a sun consumes them and they return to the stardust from whence we came. When there are no bodies, we still must find a way to remember them. For my people, the Girati, the unremembered can change a song, make it sour and out of tune, so when there were accidents or illness that made it impossible to space them, we would light a lamp, make a new star just for them, and send it off into the universe with our hopes and our dreams. Just because they bear a name, does not mean you cannot send well-wishes to those you have lost, for the dead to whom these are addressed will carry your messages to those who went before. In this way we honor them, and promise that we will never forget them."

He picked up the small shard of metal he had taken from Songbird. "What we thought was writing too badly damaged to read was, in fact, Japanese. Songbird, was a Japanese Consortium funded ship, along with others. This piece of hull, it has weight, it is permanent, unlike memory that can change or be changed. As we send our well wishes and prayers for the dead, remember the living, and the sacrifice they have made, their sons, their daughters, their fathers, their mothers, their siblings, are reflected in these names. And understand, at any time, these names could be ours. And one of them, is one of ours. Abby."

He put down the hull plate. "And one more of our own fights for his life in medical. So, as you light the lanterns remember him, and ask them, those who have gone before us, to lend him strength to hang on. To come back to us."

He lit the wick of his lamp and held it as it filled with hot air. "Each lamp bears a name, these are the names of the crew."

The door, protected by a forcefield to keep the air, opened as each of the lanterns began to float. "And we are, symbolically, giving them to the universe. So when they feel like they want to float, let them. A few have no names, just the symbol of the Nameless, the ones the stone took, and the ones the stone may still take. We remember the men and women they were, not the twisted beings they have become."

He walked among the lanterns helping people adjust wicks and light them, some not familiar with fire-makers of any sort. The captain noticed another set of lanterns in the corner. Each of them bore the mark of his ship.

"I thought you might need those for later." Jeffries said quietly. In front of him was the large lantern for Abby. "Will you help me light it?"

As the two of them lit it, it went up and when it ran into the ceiling it drifted out the open bulkhead and into space, and they watched the floating lights until they had drifted out of sight. Each of them praying or singing or sharing memories, or telling the story of the Songbird, repeating it time after time so that they could remember it and tell others. The one promise they had made. The few Girati on the ship, stood and from their places sang the song of the lament. It is a melody without words, but filled with grief and emotion, and it is how the ship as whole cries. Even the non-Girati were moved, many to tears by the song. None of them could explain it, except to wonder how human voices could make such music without words, and yet, so full of words that you understood everything.

Once the song had faded, there was silence, and then slowly, very slowly, the sound of talking began again as there were small discussions on what they heard, who they remembered, and who they prayed for. If AJ was better—when AJ was better, he would bring him here and tell him, and they would drink and light a lantern for their loved ones and maybe begin to get rid of the dangerous grief that had nearly killed them all, twice.

Quarantine Log

THE PLANETOID, HEREBY CLASSIFIED N4M31355, is hereby quarantined forever. Anyone breaking quarantine will be subject to death. Anyone bringing crystal from said planet will also be subject to death. The file for this incident is classified deep black, so any of the preceding log shall not, under any circumstances, become public knowledge in the time to which it pertains.

If, in the passage of time, all people contained herein are dead, and have no living relative to object, this project may be unsealed. The only exception being that the quarantine is broken. If that happens and the subject of the break has made it off world, then it shall be authorized by the government of the time, that Tyrell and his crew, if they be living, be tasked with using all due force necessary to return said individual to the planet aforementioned wherein to live out the rest of their days.

If the ship is unavailable, the crew disabled or dead, then it shall fall to Major Hunter of the Avengers to choose a crew to stand in their place, and they shall be authorized to read this file in toto. And heretofore will be given a Black classification befitting such classified information, and it shall remain irrevocable until such time as they have proved themselves a danger to mankind or succumbed to death, whichever might arise first.

A translation node has been imbedded into this log so that any who call it up will be able to understand it. So please, read with caution.

Further note: The governor of New Zion has been overthrown, and a new, more understanding governor has been installed in his place. While some may blame the OSU it was not, instead it was a revolution from within starting with the defense core that worked with Abby, when her name was stricken after she left, they rose up and overthrew the government with the slogan "For Abby, For Freedom!" as their battle-cry.

The clone of Jeffries was found to have been installed under the orders of the former captain of the ship, Captain Rican, and his father, Admiral Rican, both serving life sentences without the possibility of parole on Ashkur. The bombing, under further investigation, had nothing to do with the Nameless, nor did the poisoning of AJ Jones as such. These items alone will be available in the records. And all subsequent attachments. They will be known as the "Aldis" file, as there are elements that apply here, and it is specifically that incident that set in motion this attempted assassination.

Captain's Log

Captain's Log: Final.

For the first time in my long life, I forgot what it meant to be Girati. I was so wrapped up in my pain and grief that twice my decisions were compromised by that grief. If it were not for the exemplary actions of my crew, I might have made a mistake to cost me my steel. That phrase sounds so clinical in Standard, but in Girati, it is a living phrase. "Steel," ship, family, they are all the same word. Just as the word for home, and the word for ship, are the same. A long time ago, I learned the difference between a captain and a Fe'an. A Fe'an must ask himself what is best for the crew, for the steel, even if it means making a choice he doesn't like.

For his actions on this mission, I have placed a personal Commendation on Toru's file. His firm guiding hand was everything I needed from a first. And he never wavered from his devotion to me, or to the ship and crew. The planet has been quarantined, AJ is still in medical, and we are making our way to the rim to get our N space engines on. And as much as I hope that the story of the nameless dies with Songbird, I know the truth. There is a good chance, with as many as have been exposed to the crystal, that some survived.

I had been away from the song too long, not listening because of the pain, or I would have known why purple upset me so. That particular shade of purple is unique to Girati crystal, even the regular purple temporal crystal isn't that shade. That peculiar shade is only seen in a stone that has walked. A stone that has, for whatever reason, taken on a human host and walked among the ship. A thing that frightens us more than anything else.

I should also note that any psionic captains should give the planetoid a wide berth as the residual psionic energy may still be enough to control them.

Captain Tyrell Hansen,
USLS 2019